There was no time to think...

Her champagne had been drugged. The door opened. The man who stood there looked at Jessie, and his cold eyes gleamed like opals reflecting firelight. She groped for the butt of her Colt with numb and clumsy fingers. Then a blanket came down and enveloped her head. As she slid through the folds of the blanket, her right hand scraped against the stubby derringer nestled in her boot top. Jessie was clinging desperately to consciousness. She slid the wicked little derringer out...

─◆ WESLEY ELLIS ◆─

LONE STAR

AND THE RAILROAD WAR

A JOVE BOOK

LONE STAR AND THE RAILROAD WAR

A Jove Book/published by arrangement with
the author

PRINTING HISTORY
Jove edition/September 1983

ISBN: 0-515-07133-1

PRINTED IN THE UNITED STATES OF AMERICA

LONE STAR

AND THE
RAILROAD WAR

★

Chapter 1

"There are people who'd call this land a desert, Ki," Jessie Starbuck said. Her sea-green eyes swept the seemingly endless expanse of the vast prairie that surrounded them, a vista of low, broken hills and half-hidden arroyos covered with short grass that was beginning to turn yellow in the late summer heat. She tossed her head, and under the wide brim of her low-crowned hat, her shoulder-length mane of tawny hair glinted as the sun touched it. "But I call it home, and I don't think I'd ever want to live anywhere else but here, on the Circle Star."

"I've heard your father say the same thing, Jessie," Ki told her. "He loved the ranch, just as you do."

They rode on across the prairie in companionable silence, letting their horses set their own gait, feeling no need for conversation, until Ki touched the reins of his horse to slow it down. He brought a hand up to the rolled bandanna that encircled his head, and shaded his almond-shaped eyes, the most visible evidence of his Japanese ancestry.

1

"I see the line fence just ahead," he said. "But we haven't run into that bunch of stray yearlings Ed asked us to look for."

"Let's ride the line for a little way," Jessie suggested. "If we don't see them before we're ready to turn back, Ed will just have to send one of the hands out to find them tomorrow."

Jessie pressed her leg lightly against Sun's flank. The magnificent palomino turned and started moving parallel to the strands of barbwire that marked the ranch's boundary line. Ki reined his mount to follow her. They'd ridden only a short distance along the fenceline, the hot wind of mid-afternoon in their faces now, when Jessie reined in suddenly and half-rose in her stirrups, gazing at the terrain on the other side of the fence.

"Ki. Look there. It's a body."

"You're right," he agreed. He pulled up his horse and tossed the reins over its head. Like all Circle Star mounts, the animal was trained to stand when its rider trailed the reins. Ki dismounted, telling Jessie, "You wait, I'll go look. It might be unpleasant."

"Even if it is, I'd rather go with you."

Jessie let Sun's reins trail, and swung out of the saddle. She walked beside Ki to the fence. He put a hand on the nearest post and vaulted lightly over the top strand of wire, then lifted the middle strand to let Jessie duck through. They walked side by side toward the huddled form that had caught her eye.

Details became visible. The body was that of a small man wearing blue jeans and a denim shirt; a felt hat that had rolled off its wearer's head when he fell lay at one side, exposing a shock of sandy hair. Ki knelt and turned the body faceup.

"Why—it's just a boy!" Jessie exclaimed. "He's not dead, is he, Ki?"

Ki pressed the back of his hand to the youth's forehead.

2

"No. He's breathing, but he's got a high fever and his skin's tight and parched. Heat prostration."

"I'll go get the canteen," Jessie volunteered.

Ki had already lowered the youth's head and was on his feet. "I'll get it, Jessie. You stay here and shield his face from the sun with your hat."

On her knees beside the boy's recumbent figure, Jessie held her hat to shade his white, drawn face. She put his age at about fourteen or fifteen. He had not yet begun to shave, but a fuzz that was neither down nor quite whiskers grew along his jawline and a shading of the same light fuzz covered his upper lip. His cracked lips were pale, almost as light as his skin, and his aquiline nose was pinched and thin. She saw the edge of a folded paper protruding from his shirt pocket, and was reaching for it when Ki returned with the canteen.

Jessie deferred investigating the slip of paper until later. She slipped off her neckerchief, crumpled it into a wad, and held it while Ki soaked it with water from the canteen. She squeezed the sopping cloth gently, holding it over the boy's mouth, letting a few drops wet his lips and trickle down his throat, then started mopping the taut, parched skin of his face with the wet bandanna.

Ki said thoughtfully, "He isn't wearing a gunbelt, and he's got on shoes instead of boots, and his hat has a narrow brim, so it's not likely that he's a hand from one of the ranches around here. He's a little young for that, anyway. If you don't need me to help you with him, I'll do some backtracking and see what I can turn up. I don't see any hoofprints around here, but if he was riding, his horse ought to be somewhere nearby."

"Go ahead," Jessie said. "I'll be all right, I don't need any help right this minute."

After Ki left, Jessie concentrated on keeping the boy's face moistened and trickling water into his mouth a few drops at a time. Treating sunstroke was not new to her.

Even those who were accustomed to living and working in the pitiless, glaring sunshine of the southwest Texas summer occasionally misjudged the amount of exposure they'd had, and fell victim to heat prostration caused by going too long in the sun's searing rays without drinking enough water to replenish body fluids lost through sweating.

Jessie knew that she had to maintain a careful balance in restoring the liquids the sun and hot air had drained from the boy's slight body. Drinking too much water too fast brought on convulsions that could kill, but if the water that a sunstoke victim needed was not replaced rapidly enough, there was danger that an equally fatal fever would develop. She kept wetting the bandanna, mopping the face and hands of the unconscious youth and squeezing a few carefully counted drops of water into his mouth.

Ki had not yet returned when the boy stirred. His body began trembling, and after a moment he opened his eyes. He stared unseeingly into the coppery sky, and Jessie hurriedly held her hat up to shield his face from the sun. Gradually the boy's eyes lost their vacant stare. Jessie held the dripping bandanna above his mouth and squeezed out a few drops. They boy grabbed for it with feeble, uncoordinated movements of his hands, and Jessie moved it quickly out of his reach.

"Lie still," she commanded. "I know you're thirsty, but if you were to drink too much now, you'd be in worse shape than you already are. Just be quiet and let me take care of you."

A dry rasping came from the youth's throat, and his lips worked when he tried to answer her, but he could form no words with his swollen tongue. Jessie squeezed a tiny trickle of water into his mouth and he swallowed, his face twitching in pain as he moved his tongue and throat.

"Don't try to swallow," she cautioned. "Just let the water run down your throat. You'll be able to talk in a few minutes."

By now the glazed look had left the youngster's eyes.

4

He nodded that he understood, and lay quietly. Jessie kept up her ministrations, and after several more dribbles of water had gone down his throat he wheezed a bit, swallowed hard, and spoke in a hoarse, strained whisper.

"Lady," he said, "you know where the Circle Star ranch is?"

"Of course. It's—"

"I got to get there," the boy broke in, trying to sit up.

Jessie slip an arm under his shoulders to support him as she said, "Stop worrying, now. And please lie still! You're in no condition to move yet."

"How far away am I?" the youth asked. Before Jessie could reply, he went on insistently, "I got to find Mr. Alex Starbuck as fast as I can."

"He's—" Jessie stopped short. She realized suddenly that almost anything she said to the boy about Alex would only confuse and excite him, and that was the last thing he needed. She said, "You're just a few steps from the Circle Star now. That's its boundary fence, right over there."

As soon as she'd spoken, Jessie was sorry for what she'd said. The youth pulled away from her supporting arm and tried to sit up. His movement startled her, and she squeezed the bandanna involuntarily. A stream of water ran into the youth's mouth. He gagged, and his body convulsed as he coughed chokingly. The strain of coughing, combined with his struggling movements, was too much for his weakened system. His eyes rolled upward and he lapsed into unconsciousness again.

Jessie dropped the bandanna and placed her hand on the boy's chest. His heart was fluttering wildly when she first felt it, but as the seconds ticked away, it slowed to a normal, steady beat. She let the youth's shoulders down again, and propped her hat on his forehead at a slant that shaded his face from the sun; then she picked up the bandanna and brushed it clean. She was wetting it from the canteen again when Ki returned.

"How is the boy?" he asked.

5

"Better, I think. At least he was, until he tried to talk and got excited and fainted."

"He talked? What did he say?"

"He asked where the Circle Star is, Ki! He came here looking for my dad!"

"Why?"

"I don't know why! He fainted before he could tell me."

Ki nodded thoughtfully. "That fits in with what I figured out while I was backtracking."

"What do you mean?" Jessie frowned.

"I only meant that I figured out he was heading for the ranch, Jessie. I backtracked his footprints as far as the ridges just this side of the road, and even from the top of the highest ridge I didn't see any sign of a horse."

"Where could he have started from?" Jessie asked, her brow wrinkling into a puzzled frown. "All there is in that direction is the railroad. Ki, you don't think—"

"Yes, I do, Jessie," Ki broke in. "The railroad station's the only place he could have come from. You know how the road curves to avoid the ridges. The stationmaster probably headed him this way in a straight line, to save him five or six miles of walking along the road."

"But that's still fifteen miles, Ki! It's almost a full day's walk. No wonder he got sunstroke!"

"He's lucky we came along when we did."

"Yes." Jessie looked at the boy's face. It was pallid and drawn, though he was breathing regularly and steadily. She took the slip of paper protruding from his shirt pocket, and unfolded it. A frown formed on her face as she looked up at Ki and said, "All that's written down here is 'Circle Star Ranch, Sarah County, Texas.'"

"That's probably all the address he had, and he didn't want to forget the name of the county," Ki suggested.

"I suppose. But why did he ask for Alex, Ki? Wouldn't anyone who knows the Circle Star know that my father's been dead all these years?"

6

"Not necessarily. Not if they came from a place far enough away so they'd have to travel here by train."

"I suppose." She looked down at the youth's colorless face. "Ki, we'd better get him to the house. He's not showing any signs of coming around, and he ought to be out of this hot sun."

"We can carry him to the horses. It's only a few steps."

Between them, they got the unconscious youth to the fence, and slid him under the bottom strand of barbwire. When they reached the horses, Ki mounted up and lifted the boy by the arms while Jessie boosted his legs. When the boy was settled into the front of the saddle, Ki wrapped an arm around the youth's chest and they started back to the Circle Star's main house.

Ed Wright, the Circle Star foreman, was working at the horse corral and saw them approaching. He was waiting when they reined in, and helped them get the still unconscious youth into the house.

"Where'd you find him?" Wright asked Ki as they laid the boy on the bed in the room adjoining Jessie's. "He's not from around here, judging by the outfit he's wearing."

"I had the same idea," Ki said, as he and Wright began undressing the unconscious lad. "He was lying on the prairie, just outside the line fence on the north range."

Jessie entered the room in time to hear Ki's reply. She'd let Ki and the foreman carry the boy to the room while she got a pail of water and a stack of large bath towels. Unfolding one of the towels while she spoke, she told Wright, "We don't know anything about him yet, Ed, except that he asked where he could find the Circle Star, and then said he was looking for Alex."

"But your father—" Wright began.

Ki interrrupted. "Yes. The boy didn't know Alex was dead, so that means he's not from anyplace near here."

Jessie spread the water-soaked towel over the recumbent youth, covering him from shoulders to knees. Over her

7

shoulder she asked, "Did you look in his pockets?"

"Not yet." Ki picked up the boy's trousers and emptied the pockets. He said, "Three cartwheels and a few pennies. A jackknife and a piece of string. And the paper that was in his shirt pocket. That's all, and it certainly isn't much."

Jessie had placed her palm on the boy's forehead after she'd covered him. She said, "His fever seems to be going down. I think we got to him just in time, Ki. A little while longer in that sun, and he might not have come around."

Jessie's touch had aroused the youth. He stirred and opened his eyes. For a moment he gazed into space, disoriented. He stared at the ceiling without moving, then turned his head slowly while he looked around the room. After examining his surroundings, he fixed his eyes on Jessie, Ki, and Ed.

"You don't have anything to worry about," Jessie assured him, her voice soothing. "You're at the Circle Star ranch, and after you've rested awhile you can tell us who you are, and then we'll talk about why you came here."

"If this is the Circle Star, where's Mr. Alex Starbuck?" the boy demanded. His voice was still very weak, and he spoke in a rasping half-whisper.

"Let's talk about that later," Jessie said. "Unless you'd like to tell me why you came here. I'm Jessie Starbuck."

"Mr. Alex Starbuck's wife?"

"No. His daughter."

"I guess I better wait," he said. "Grandpa always told me if there was trouble too big for him to handle, he could get Mr. Starbuck to help him."

"Who is your grandfather?" Jessie asked.

"Captain Bob Tinker. You'd oughta know that, if you're Mr. Starbuck's girl."

"I suppose there are a lot of things I don't know," Jessie replied. "Including your name."

"It's Bobby. After Grandpa."

"Where do you live, Bobby?"

"With Grandpa, of course. In Hidden Valley."

Bobby's voice was growing raspy again. Jessie filled a glass with water from the pitcher that stood on the marble-topped commode beside the bed. She handed him the water, but he was unable to close his hand around the glass.

Jessie slid her arm under Bobby's shoulders, lifted him a bit, held the glass to his lips, and let him drink a few sips. He groped for the glass, trying to grasp it and empty it in a few quick gulps, but Jessie quickly moved it out of his reach. Even this slight exertion was too much for the weakened youth. He sagged back onto the bed, and Jessie slid her arm away and let him fall back with his head on the pillow.

"You've got to rest now, Bobby," she said gently. "We can talk later about you and your grandfather, and why he sent you here to find Alex Starbuck."

"I ain't got time to rest!" Bobby said, his face contorting into a worried frown. "I got to find Mr. Starbuck and tell . . . tell him . . . Grandpa's in . . . trouble."

Bobby's last few words trailed off and were almost inaudible as his body sagged and his eyes closed and he lost consciousness again. Jessie placed a hand on his forehead as she and the men stood looking at the youth's towel-draped form.

"He's all right," Jessie assured them. "Just very weak. He'll sleep awhile, and I imagine he needs food. We haven't any way of knowing how long it's been since he ate last."

"Did anything he said make sense to you, Jessie?" Ki asked.

Jessie shook her head. "I was hoping you'd understand it."

"I remember hearing your father mention Captain Tinker a few times," Ki said. "But all I can recall is the name."

"There are probably some entries in his old diaries that will give us a clue," Jessie said. "I'll see what I can find, after supper."

"Do you think I'd better stay here and keep an eye on Bobby?" Ki asked.

"He won't need anyone with him while he's asleep, Ki," Jessie replied. "It's safe to leave him by himself for a while. I'll come in and change the towels every hour or so, to get some moisture back into his system. All he really needs besides that is rest, and food as soon as he can eat it."

Jessie sighed as she placed the pocket-sized, black-bound book she'd just leafed through on top of the three she'd skimmed earlier. She leaned back in the big leather-upholstered chair that had been her father's favorite, and closed her eyes. The chair had become her favorite, too, for it still bore the faint fragrance of Alex Starbuck's cherry-flavored pipe tobacco.

Jessie did not allow herself a long relaxation. On the table beside the chair were two stacks of Alex's early diaries. The four books in the smaller stack were the ones she'd skimmed through since suppertime, and there were seven in the stack she'd not yet touched. She took the book that was on top of the larger stack and began leafing through it, reading rapidly, looking for the name of Captain Tinker.

She'd thumbed through three books before she found the name, and then the entry was nothing more than a bare mention of Tinker as the skipper of a ship called the *Sea Sprite,* which had carried some of Alex's cargoes of Oriental merchandise from the Far East to San Francisco, in the early days of his importing business. Finding the name in the fourth book had encouraged her, but as she started on the one she'd just picked up, the mantel clock struck ten, reminding her that it was time to look in on Bobby Tinker again.

Laying the diary aside, Jessie went through the spacious living room and mounted the stairs. She'd left a night light in the hallway, and at the corridor's end she noted that the door to Ki's bedroom was closed, as were all the others except the bedroom where Bobby Tinker lay, which she'd left ajar. She went in and looked at the youth.

He was still sleeping peacefully. Jessie felt his forehead

10

and found that his fever was almost gone. She took a fresh wet towel from the pail beside the bed and spread it over him after removing the one that had covered him before. The windows of the room were open, and the breeze that had been warm when she'd changed the towels an hour earlier was beginning to blow cooler. Jessie stepped to the windows to pull them down, and stood for a moment looking out over the sleeping ranch.

As they did on any ranch, days began before sunrise on the Circle Star, and bedtime came immediately after supper. The bunkhouse and cookshack that stood beyond the corrals loomed dark and silent in the moonless night. In the square enclosed by the pole fence, she could see the horses standing quietly.

Jessie was reaching up to close the window when a flicker of motion at the corner of the cookshack caught her eyes. She let her arms down slowly and stood watching. A shadowy form, then another, and finally a third moved away from the cookshack and toward the corrals. Jessie wasted no time. The figures were not those of any Circle Star hands, or there'd have been a light in the bunkhouse. She closed the door of the bedroom as she left, and went down the hall to Ki's door.

"Ki!" she called softly, tapping the door's panels with her fingertips.

"Jessie?" Ki replied. In a moment the door opened and Ki was at her side. "What's wrong?"

"We have some unwanted visitors. They're at the corral now, coming toward the house."

"Give me a minute, I'll get my jacket and *bo*."

"I'll be in the hall downstairs," Jessie said.

Hurrying now, she went down the steps and through the big living room. She took a rifle from the rack that was affixed to the wall just inside the door, and stood waiting for Ki to join her.

Chapter 2

"How many of them are there?" Ki asked when he stopped inside the front door where Jessie stood. He leaned his *bo* against the wall while he finished buttoning his jacket.

"I saw three, Ki. They were going from the cookhouse to the corrals. There may be others that I couldn't see in the dark."

"Suppose you cover me from the veranda," Ki suggested. "If there are only three, I can handle them."

"No. It's too dark. If I have to shoot, I might hit you by mistake."

"I've got more confidence in your shooting than you have," Ki said, smiling. "It wouldn't be like you to hit a target you're not aiming at."

Jessie returned Ki's smile, but said, "We'll go together, Ki. You lead. I'll back you up."

Ki nodded. He pointed to the study door, still ajar and spilling light into the living room. Jessie went to close it. As soon as the room was dark, she heard the soft click of the latch on the front door as Ki opened it. She hurried across the big room to join him. Outside, she found Ki still standing on the wide veranda, waiting for his eyes to adjust to the darkness.

"Do you see them?" Jessie whispered.

"One of them is standing at the corner of the front horse corral. I haven't spotted the others yet."

Jessie strained her eyes into the night's black gloom, which was lighted only by starshine. Beside the corral, the figure of a crouching man slowly took form. The darkness was too deep for her to distinguish anything except his figure, but she caught the glint of starshine reflected from the polished blue metal of the long-barreled gun in his hands.

"Be careful, Ki," she breathed softly. "That might be a shotgun he's holding."

"I can see it," Ki replied. "It's a rifle. They're here on some kind of dirty business, all right, and they're not horse thieves, or they'd have the corral opened by now."

"Do you see the other two?" Jessie asked.

"No, but—" Ki broke off as the man at the corner of the corral started moving toward the house.

"Where could they have gone?" Jessie frowned. "Unless the others are behind the house."

"They probably are," Ki replied. "Looking for a back door or an open window."

Neither Ki nor Jessie thought of rousing the men sleeping in the bunkhouse. Both of them had reached the same conclusion at the same time as soon as they realized the intruders were making the house their target.

"We'd better—" Jessie began.

"Yes," Ki broke in. Like Jessie, he kept his eyes on the moving man while he spoke. "I'll reduce the odds against us by keeping this one from joining his friends. But I don't want to make any noise, so I can't risk getting close enough to use my *bo*."

Ki stepped off the veranda, taking a *shuriken* from his jacket pocket as he moved. In the black jacket and trousers

13

he wore, he was an almost invisible shadow in the blackness, and his rope-soled slippers made only the faintest whisper of sound as he started toward the prowler.

Jessie followed Ki down the steps and stood watching. She released the safety of the Winchester she was holding ready. The well-oiled mechanism made a metallic click that would have been inaudible only a few paces away.

She watched as Ki angled in the direction of the corral to intercept the intruder, and saw the bright polished metal of the *shuriken* glinting in the starlight as it whirled silently and swiftly to its target. The prowler's breath rushed from his lungs in a strangled gasp when the razor-keen edges of the star-pointed throwing disc sliced into his throat. Then, as he involuntarily raised his hands to grasp the silent weapon that was draining away his life's blood, the man let his rifle fall.

A shout sounded from behind the ranch house when the gun hit the hard ground with a night-shattering clatter. Jessie started running along the front of the house, toward Ki. Boot soles gritted on the sunbaked soil, and almost instantly gunfire blasted away the night's silence as a dark figure rushed from behind the end of the veranda and let off a shot at Ki.

Ki had anticipated the counterattack. He hit the ground as soon as he heard the man begin moving, and was rolling toward Jessie, a dark streak against the light earth, when she brought up her rifle and returned the prowler's fire.

Jessie aim was better than the intruder's had been. The dark figure crumpled to the ground, a rifle falling from his lifeless hands and thudding to the earth as the gun and the man who'd fired it dropped at the same time.

A moment of silence passed, then the noise of more running footsteps from behind the house broke the already shattered stillness. Ki was on his feet by now, and Jessie's movement had brought her to within a yard of him.

"That's the third man!" Ki said. "Quick, Jessie! If we

14

can take him alive, maybe we can get some answers out of him!"

They rounded the edge of the veranda, straining their eyes to pierce the shrouding darkness. Jessie saw the running man first. He'd evidently started running when he saw the second of his two companions fall, and had taken a course that took him away from the house at an angle.

He had already covered enough distance to take him out of reach of Ki's *shuriken*. Jessie hesitated, holding her fire momentarily, waiting for Ki to launch one of his throwing blades. Ki made no move, and Jessie realized that the time for silence had ended with her first shot, but by then the fleeing intruder was a dim shadow in the distance. She brought up the Winchester and fired, but the thudding of the running man's footsteps did not falter. When she tried to get him in her sights again, he'd vanished in the enshrouding night.

"I'm sorry, Ki," she said. "I should have shot sooner."

"No. I shouldn't have thought about trying to take him alive. What I said threw you off."

To Jessie and Ki, the fracas with the prowlers had seemed to last a long time, but actually less than two minutes had passed since the first shot broke the night's quiet, and a light was just now showing through the bunkhouse windows. The door burst open a few moments after Jessie's last shot sounded, and the men of the Circle Star came roiling out.

Only one or two of the last to emerge had taken time to pull on boots or jeans; most of the men wore only their long underwear. Ed Wright and the others who came out first had not even stopped to jam their feet into their boots. Those who were bootless ran two or three steps, slowed down when the rough ground began to hurt their bare feet, and stopped when they recognized Jessie and Ki, and heard no more shooting.

Wright held a lantern in his left hand, but the Colt he

15

gripped in his right hand had kept him from lighting it. The other cowhands also carried either revolvers or rifles. They stood in a ragged group at the edge of the area of yellow lamplight that seeped through the open door of the bunkhouse, peering into the darkness beyond Ki and Jessie, looking for a target.

"It's all over, Ed!" Jessie called. "Your boys won't need those guns."

Wright answered with a question. "You and Ki are both all right, ain't you?" He handed the lantern to one of the men who had on both jeans and boots. "Here. Light it."

"Neither of us got a scratch, Ed," Ki replied.

"What in Sam Hill started the fracas?" Wright asked.

"Jessie was looking out the window and saw a man prowling around the corral," Ki told the foreman. "She called to me and we came out to investigate. The rest of it just *happened*."

By this time the hand with the lantern had struck a match and touched it to the wick. He held it up, and its wide circle of illumination showed the body of the intruder who'd fallen nearest the corral.

"There's one of 'em, on the ground there!" the cowhand holding the lantern called out.

"There was three shots," another of the men said. "Was this dead hombre the only one you-all seen?"

"No. There were two more," Jessie replied. "One of them is lying just past the corner of the house. The third one got away."

"You want us to saddle up and take after him, Miss Jessie?" Wright asked.

Jessie shook her head. "Trying to follow him in the dark would be time wasted, Ed. I'm sure he had a horse close by."

"Horse thieves, you guess?" the foreman frowned.

Ki answered him. "They could've been, Ed. We didn't stop to ask them. We knew they weren't any of your boys, so we didn't hesitate to go after them."

16

"Sure." The foreman nodded. "They're bound to've been up to something crooked. Honest men would've knocked and said what their business was."

"Your men can clean things up, Ed," Jessie told Wright. "I'll leave that up to you."

"No use putting if off," Wright said. He looked around at the hands. "Big Bill, you take the boys who've got their boots on and move the bodies down behind the corral. We'll wait till it's daylight to do the burying." He turned back to Jessie and went on, "If you don't mind, I'm going back and put on my boots and jeans. This rough ground sorta bites into a man's feet."

"I'll go along with the men and take a look at the bodies," Ki told Jessie. "Do you want to come along?"

She shook her head. "No. I'm sure we've never seen them before. I'll wait at the house."

Led by the lantern-bearer, the three other men who wore boots started toward the nearest corpse. Ki joined them. He hunkered down beside the dead man and studied his face. As he'd expected, it was strange to him.

"Have any of you ever seen him before?" he asked.

One by one, the quartet of cowhands disclaimed any knowledge of the corpse's identity. Ki searched the dead man's pockets. In addition to a sack of Bull Durham, a packet of cigarette papers, and some matches, they held four gold eagles and some silver. Standing up, Ki led the men to the spot where the second body lay. None of the Circle Star hands could identify this corpse either. When Ki repeated his search, the results were much the same; the dead man's pockets yielded chewing tobacco instead of cigarette makings, but they also held four gold eagles and an almost identical amount in silver.

"Now that just ain't natural," one of the cowhands said thoughtfully. "Everybody I know's got all kinds of truck stuck in his jeans pockets, like a knife and a spare bandanna and maybe a letter or two from home and some kind of personal stuff."

17

"You're right about that, Bishop," Ki agreed. "Someone told these men to be sure they didn't carry anything that would help identify them if they got caught."

"Or killed," one of the other hands put in.

"Or killed," Ki echoed. He stood up. "You men know what to do. It's Ed's job from here on."

Ki went to join Jessie. She'd opened the study door to let the light flood the living room, and was replacing her rifle on the rack by the door. Ki shook his head in reply to the unspoken question that was in her eyes when she turned to face him.

"Strangers," he said. "Nothing in their pockets except some money. An almost identical amount of money, in fact. Four eagles and a few dollars in silver. Does that lead you to the same conclusion I reached?"

"I think I knew they were cartel killers from the beginning, Ki," she answered in a quiet voice. "What you said about the money just confirms what I suspected when they didn't try to steal the horses. They were given fifty dollars each in advance, probably promised another fifty when they brought Bobby Tinker back, or reported they'd killed him."

"Yes. That's my idea too."

"Speaking of Bobby, I'd better look in on him." Jessie started up the stairs, Ki following. She added, "The shooting may have roused him, and worry is the last thing he needs."

"I suppose they trailed him from the railroad," Ki said as they went up the stairs. "They'd have been given the layout of the ranch, of course, in case they didn't catch up with him before he got here."

"I'm sure the cartel has a set of very detailed maps of the Circle Star," Jessie said.

There was bitterness in her voice, for her words recalled all too vividly the black day when Alex Starbuck had died under a hail of bullets from the repeating guns of the cartel's hired assassins. Until that day, Alex had fought successfully all the efforts made by the corrupt European-based cabal to take over the industrial empire he'd built on the base of a

18

small San Francisco store selling goods imported from the Orient.

At the time of his death, Alex's holdings had expanded to include either full control of or large investments in shipping, railroads, mining, foundries, banking, and other, smaller enterprises. It was this vast structure, as well as the Circle Star, that had been Jessie's inheritance from her father, just as had been his unflagging war with the cartel. Ki had served Alex, and had transferred his allegiance to Jessie after her father's murder.

"Speaking of details," Ki said as they reached the door of Bobby Tinker's room, "did you find anything helpful in Alex's diaries?"

"Just one short mention of Captain Tinker and his ship, the *Sea Sprite*. But I still have several more to go through."

Jessie opened the door of the room a crack. The soft glow of the lamp in the hall sent a shaft of light through the slit, and she saw Bobby sitting up in bed, the coverlet draped around his shoulders.

"Bobby!" she exclaimed, opening the door fully. "You shouldn't be sitting up yet!"

"I heard guns going off. I was scared. What happened?"

"There were some men prowling around," Jessie said. "They may have been after our horses."

"What horses?"

"Our ranch horses. Don't you remember, Bobby? I'm Jessie Starbuck, and you're at the Circle Star ranch."

"I didn't remember right off, when the shooting woke me up," the boy said. "But I do now." He pointed to Ki. "Who's he?"

"This is Ki. He'll be your friend too, just like I will, if you'll let us."

Bobby studied Ki's face for a moment, then nodded slowly. "I guess I will. But where's Mr. Alex Starbuck? He's the one I came to find. Grandpa needs help real bad."

"We'll talk about that in a minute," Jessie promised. "The first thing to do is to get you settled back in bed."

19

She spent a moment rearranging the covers after Bobby lay down, then said, "Now before we talk about helping your grandpa, wouldn't you like something to eat? You must be hungry."

"I guess I am, some," Bobby replied. "I feel sorta funny all over. Not as much as when I woke up. But when the guns stopped going off and I used the chamberpot, I felt better."

"I'll see what I can find in the kitchen," Ki volunteered.

When Ki had gone, Jessie sat down on the bed. "Bobby, Alex Starbuck was my father, and he's dead."

Jessie watched the boy's face carefully. Bobby swallowed hard, but, as with any youth brought up on the frontier, death to him was a fact to be accepted stoically. His eyes widened and she saw his face beginning to pucker into a disappointed frown.

She went on quickly, "Perhaps Ki and I can help your grandfather, but we'll have to find out what kind of trouble he's in. Suppose you tell me about it."

For a moment or two, Bobby was silent, his frown deepening. Then he said, "If Mr. Starbuck was your daddy, I guess he told you about him and Grandpa sailing all over the ocean together."

"He didn't exactly tell me, but I know a little bit about it," Jessie answered. "Your grandfather used to be the captain of a ship called the *Sea Sprite,* didn't he?"

Bobby nodded. "He brought things to San Francisco for Mr. Starbuck, all kinds of stuff from China and Japan and places like that. Sometimes Mr. Starbuck was on Grandpa's ship with him."

"Yes." Jessie nodded. "I know a little about that."

"They fought pirates together sometimes," Bobby went on, his eyes opening wider. "And I guess Grandpa done a lot to help Mr. Starbuck, because when Grandpa got hurt and couldn't be a ship captain any more, Mr. Starbuck gave him some land in Nevada Territory. Grandma was still alive then, and my daddy was just a little boy, but he's dead

20

too, now. Went East to fight in the War, and never came home. So some of Grandma's and Grandpa's folks too, from back East, they came out to live with Grandpa on his land."

"This was the land my father had given him?" Jessie asked when Bobby ran out of breath and stopped.

"Yes, ma'am. Well, everything's been fine in Hidden Valley until just a—"

"Wait, Bobby," Jessie broke in. "This land my father gave your grandfather is called Hidden Valley?"

Bobby nodded again. "It's called that because it's sorta separated from everyplace else by the foothills."

"What foothills?"

"Why, the Sierra foothills. Hidden Valley's way over west in Nevada Territory, right close to California."

"All right, I understand now," Jessie told him. "Go on."

"There's some men that want to build a railroad through the valley," Bobby said. "But they need a lot of land for their tracks, and some of the folks don't want to sell their land because it'd break up their farms, and some of them would have to leave their houses, and all like that. So the railroad people are mad, and the folks in Hidden Valley are mad, and there's all sorts of trouble starting."

"And you'd heard your grandfather say that if he ever got into trouble and needed help, he knew Alex Starbuck would help him?"

"Yes, ma'am. Mama heard him say that too, and she told Grandpa he better ask Mr. Starbuck for help before it was too late. And Grandpa always says it's not that bad yet. So I sorta figured that if he wasn't going to do anything, and Mama wasn't going to do anything, I'd better."

Jessie said slowly, "Bobby, I don't suppose you told your mother or your grandfather that you were going to ask for help?"

Bobby shook his head emphatically. "I sure didn't! Because if I'd of told 'em, they'd of said no!"

"How did you know where to come and look for my father?"

21

"Grandpa's talked about Mr. Alex Starbuck ever since I can remember. I wasn't real sure where this ranch was, so I sorta asked him a few questions, and started out."

"What did you do for money?"

"I work and earn my own money, Miss Starbuck. I didn't have to ask anybody for help. I hitched some rides on wagons along the way through the valley and rode the stage coach some and got to the Santa Fe railroad. The ticket seller figured out where I had to change trains to get the rest of the way. And I got here, didn't I?"

"Yes, you did, But you came very close to not making it." When Bobby did not answer, Jessie went on, "What did you expect my father to do for your grandfather, Bobby?"

"I—I guess I ain't sure. But Grandpa said so many times how certain he was Mr. Alex Starbuck would help him—" The youth stopped short, his lower lip quivering. "I guess I made a mistake, didn't I? I ought to of found out more before I left. I didn't know Mr. Starbuck was dead."

"Sometimes news doesn't travel very fast, Bobby. Even bad news." Jessie sat silent for a moment, then she asked the boy, "I guess you know what 'inheritance' means, don't you?"

"Why—it means something that's passed along in a family, like a house or money, I suppose."

"Or an obligation," she added. "No Bobby, even if I don't quite approve of the way you went about things, you haven't made a mistake coming here. From what you've told me, I'm sure Alex would have helped your grandfather."

"You mean you're going to—"

"Of course. I always try to do what Alex would have done himself, Bobby. We'll have to talk some more, and you need to rest a few days. But Ki and I will go back to Hidden Valley with you and and see what we can do to help your grandpa get things straightened out."

Chapter 3

West of the rutted road over which the lurching, bumping stagecoach was traveling, the land rose steeply in a single breathtaking upward sweep to the towering crests of the pine-covered Sierra Nevadas; to the east, it stretched in a slowly lifting expanse of arid semidesert to the low, broken humps of the barren Wassuk Range.

Since they'd left the comparatively comfortable seats in the swaying passenger coach of the Santa Fe Railroad at Kingman, Jessie, Ki, and Bobby had jounced and bounced constantly in one or another of several stagecoaches they'd boarded. They'd changed vehicles in tiny towns: Eldorado, Potosi, Reville, Columbus, Belleville, and, most recently, Aurora.

Jessie thought as they traveled that the towns must have been bitterly disappointing to the first miners and prospectors who had named them out of hopes and dreams and memories. In most of the new communities there had been a few good years, then the lodes had begun to peter out, and the same men who'd established them had moved on to look for new and bigger strikes. The number of passengers traveling on the stage line gauged the decline of the towns; when the coach pulled out of Aurora, Jessie and Ki and Bobby were its only occupants.

After starting north from Kingman, the stage had passed one heavy freightwagon after another hauling rails and ties north, but it was not until they left Aurora and started up the shallow valley between the Sierras and the Wassuks that they'd seen any actual track laid by the South Sierra Railway Company. The rails were still new, not yet worn shiny, unused by anything heavier than handcars. Several of these had whizzed past the slower stagecoach, with two men pumping the handles while a half-dozen others balanced precariously on the crowded platform.

"Isn't this a strange way to build a railroad, Jessie?" Ki asked as they watched one of the handcars disappear. "From everything I've heard, the rails are usually laid from each end of the line to meet in the middle, but this South Sierra Railway outfit is starting in the middle and building to each end."

"I don't know much about building railroads, Ki," she said. "But from what Bobby's told us, they're also laying rails south to Hidden Valley and north to the Southern Pacific mainline."

"That's right," Bobby chimed in. "Grandpa says they want to get the big shipments out of the mines up north of the valley, at places like Washoe City and Como and Virginia City."

"Well, that makes sense, at least," Ki said. "And I suppose there's a reason for it, but it seems to me they're counting a lot on getting the right-of-way through Hidden Valley."

"Grandpa says that, too," Bobby nodded. "He says us folks in Hidden Valley have got the railroad promoters in a bind. If they can't buy the land through those passes at

24

the north and south ends of the valley, he says they'll have to spend a mint of money putting their tracks through the mountains."

"If the country around Hidden Valley is anything like what we're looking at now, I'd agree with your grandpa," Jessie said.

"It's pretty much the same," Bobby told her. "Lots of ups and downs every place you look."

Jessie didn't say that the geography of the valley was no surprise to her. Before they'd started from the Circle Star, after having given Bobby a few days of rest to recover from his sunstroke, she'd finished reading Alex Starbuck's early diaries. In them she'd found entries explaining why her father had felt so indebted to Captain Tinker; the entries had also revealed the acute perceptions that had made Starbuck so successful.

"At midnight, a day out of Tientsin in the Chingchan Strait, boarded by Chinese pirates," Alex had written in his copperplate script, the words as legible as the day he'd put them down, though the oxgall ink he'd used had faded to a pale purple-tan. *"Capt. Tinker at helm, mates and crew belowdecks when pirates attacked. Luckily, I was in my cabin, so I could get to deck to help Tinker. Exhausted pistol ammunition, and Tinker fought to me with cutlass, after suffering grievous sword-slash in thigh. Except for Tinker, I would not have survived the fight and my cargo would have been lost."*

In another diary, of a later year, she read: *"Visited Capt. Tinker, found him in deplorable situation. He was forced to sell the* Sea Sprite *as the wound received from pirates when he saved my life now prevents him following his profession. Have decided to give him Hidden Valley land for which I outbid the cartel. While the passes at each end of the valley are the only ones in a hundred miles suitable for a railroad line, I have no need for them until my railroad ventures reach the stage where the line I plan can be built. Hidden Valley has enough good farmland to allow Tinker*

25

to support himself by selling what he cannot use himself, and when the day comes to build my railroad, I can rely on Tinker to let me put its rail through the passes."

A final entry in the same diary told of Alex taking the Captain to Hidden Valley and showing it to him, then delivering the deed to Tinker. Jessie did not search through the later diaries. From the three entries she'd read, she could understand why her father had given Hidden Valley to Captain Tinker, and why Tinker would feel that if he needed help, he could turn to Alex.

"I can understand a lot more than that, of course," she'd said to Ki when telling him of the diary entries. "Alex outbid the cartel for Hidden Valley when he was competing with them during the time he was first investing in railroads. They must have records too, but even without records, some of them would remember the valley and the passes."

"They'd remember how your father beat them, too," Ki had reminded her. "The cartel never forgets or forgives a defeat. The feeling you had when Bobby first showed up was right, it seems. The South Sierra Railway Company is just another name for the cartel. We'll go help Captain Tinker fight them, of course."

"Of course," Jessie had replied, and the matter was settled.

Now, jouncing along in the stagecoach on the last leg of their journey to Hidden Valley, Jessie could appreciate her father's vision even more. Looking at the rugged mountains to the east and west, she could see where a route across level land such as the valley floor would make the passes at each of its ends a prize almost beyond price.

Ahead of the stage, Jessie saw a huddle of buildings lining the road, and as they drew closer to them, she recognized them as the railhead supply camp. On one side there were new and well-built structures; these were offices for the construction bosses, and storage buildings for tools and supplies. The buildings were flanked by stacks of ties and rails, and away from these at a little distance stood

26

corrals for the oxen and mules that pulled the big freight-wagons.

On the other side of the road stood a motley miscellany of other buildings, most of them shabby, some fairly substantial, but many only false fronts with tents behind their façades. Some had identifying signs: rooming houses and restaurants, saloons, gambling houses, and a few stores. Some had no signs, but were easy to recognize; they were cribs for the whores who, like the gamblers, swarmed where men had money and few places to spend it.

Jessie had seen similar shantytowns at other railheads, and remembered that the shanties moved with the rails. Many of them were even designed to be moved, built on sturdy timbers to which wagon wheels could be attached. This feature and the predatory character of their inhabitants had been combined in the name by which construction crews called them wherever railroads were being built: Hell on Wheels.

At that hour in midafternoon, Hell on Wheels had not yet come to life, and the road was deserted on the side the shantytown occupied. The opposite side was as active as a disturbed anthill. Men hurried between the buildings, and crews of laborers loaded supplies on the big freight wagons—not only ties and steel rails, but spikes and fishplates, sacks of nuts and bolts and wrenches, mauls, shovels, sledgehammers, all the materials needed by the tracklaying crews up the line.

Ki was sitting beside the window on the right-hand side of the coach, Jessie on the left side, and since there were no other passengers, Bobby was occupying the seat facing them so that he could slide from window to window and watch whatever interested him in the area through which they were passing.

Ki's interest had been caught by the activity in the supply yard. He saw a big flatbed wagon, piled high with a load of crossties, pull out of a loading area just ahead of the stagecoach and start for the road, and he noticed that it was

27

being drawn by a team of horses instead of the more usual mules or oxen. He wondered why, then some other movement elsewhere in the yard caught his eye and he looked away from the wagon.

His attention was drawn back to the horsedrawn freightwagon by the flickering whip the teamster on its seat was wielding. The loaded wagon was moving along one of the lanes that had been left between the heaps of supplies at right angles to the road, to give the freightwagons access and loading space. In spite of its heavy load, the wagon was gaining speed rapidly, and the distance between it and the road was not great.

Ki wondered how the teamster was going to turn his horses into the road at such a speed, and instinct led him to gauge the distance between the team and the road. Experience told him instantly that unless the teamster reined in, the wagon and the stagecoach would reach the intersection at the same time.

Ki watched as the gap narrowed, but the teamster still did not pull in. Instead, he whipped his horses to a faster pace. Ki realized then that he had no time to waste. The freighter was obviously intending to drive full-tilt into the stagecoach, and apparently the man handling the stagecoach reins had not noticed the danger looming ahead.

"Jessie! Bobby!" Ki called. "Grab the catch-straps and hang on!"

Without waiting to see whether they followed his order, Ki thrust his head and shoulders out of the stagecoach window and got his feet on the seat. He levered his body up until he was half inside and half outside the vehicle, his arms stretching up its side while his hands groped for a hold on the baggage rack on the coach's roof. He got a precarious grip on the rail and hauled himself up. The stagecoach driver turned in his seat, gaping at Ki's sudden appearance.

Ki had no time to explain to the driver. He was swaying back and forth, still on his knees, trying to keep his balance

28

on top of the swaying, jouncing coach and at the same time get on his feet. The freightwagon was near the intersection now, only a dozen yards separating the lead horses from the stagecoach.

Suddenly the freightwagon's teamster hauled on the off-rein, causing his team to veer sharply to the right, out of the path of the stage. As soon as the team began turning, he released the reins and yanked sharply at a rope he'd been holding.

Ki saw the linchpin that held the wagon tongue to the axle fly through the air at the rope's end. The teamster jumped from his seat, rolling to lessen the jolt of his landing as he hit the ground. The driverless wagon kept moving swiftly ahead, a massive juggernaut now only a few feet away from the stagecoach and rolling at high speed with its heavy load of wooden ties.

With only seconds to spare, Ki found his balance atop the stagecoach. Leaning forward, he stretched out one hand to grab the reins from the stagecoach driver while, with the other hand, he pulled the long tasseled whip from its socket and lashed the backs of the stage horses with quick, flailing strokes.

Stung and surprised, the team responded to Ki's frantic lashing with a mighty jump. The high-bodied coach swayed and tilted and almost overturned, but the team's final frantic jump had pulled it clear. The freightwagon thundered past behind it, missing the stage by inches.

Careening ahead, the wagon rolled across the road and, with a thunderous impact and a splintering of boards, crashed into the front of a saloon in Hell on Wheels.

Ki did not turn his head to see the effects of the crash. He had dropped the whip and was sawing on the reins with both hands, trying to pull up the panicked team, which the noise of the crash had spooked even worse than had his whiplashing.

For a few moments the fate of the stagecoach was uncertain, but Ki managed to stay on his feet and keep a firm pressure on the reins, and the horses at last responded to the familiar command. They calmed down and finally came to a halt.

Ki tossed the reins to the dumbfounded driver. "Just hold them at a stand!" he shouted, his eyes fixed on the freighter who'd been handling the freightwagon, and who was just getting to his feet.

Launching himself from the top of the stage, Ki flexed his legs to absorb the shock of his landing and started running for the man who'd tried to crash his wagon into the stagecoach. The teamster saw him coming and whipped out his sheath knife. He spread his legs and dropped into the crouch that experienced knife-fighters favor, holding the nine-inch blade low, weaving it at waist level in a series of figure-eights.

Ki was armed with his own knife, but he left the slender, curved blade in its waistband sheath. He was confident that his skill with a blade was equal or superior to that of the man who stood waiting for him, but Ki wanted to do more than merely take his opponent alive; he wanted to humiliate the man by defeating him without using a weapon.

"You better back away before you get hurt, Chink," the freighter said tauntingly. When Ki came on without hesitating, the man added, "All right, yellowbelly! I warned you once! Now you got no excuse when I slice you up in little pieces!"

Giving no indication that he'd heard the teamster's warning, Ki pressed on. The freighter lunged at him, bringing his knife up in a slashing thrust, its point aimed at Ki's abdomen.

Ki turned his body an instant before the blade reached him, and instead of reversing his turn to face his adversary, he spun around with dazzling speed and at the same time brought down the edge of his hand with a slashing stroke that landed on the freighter's forearm just above the wrist, where sensitive nerves lie across the bone with no protective sheath of muscle tissue.

His arm numbed by the blow, the teamster opened his hand involuntarily. His knife fell to the ground while Ki's body was still only halfway through its turn.

As he spun around on his right foot, Ki extended his left leg, bringing his foot up to shoulder height and snapping his heel forward just as he completed the turn. Ki delivered his kick with the force of a bludgeon, and heard the evidence that it had struck its intended target when the man's collarbone broke with a loud pop.

For a second or two, while the teamster began crumpling to the ground, his arm dangling uselessly, Ki stood with his leg still upraised, watching the mingled look of pain and surprise that contorted his attacker's face. Then he lowered his foot and stood with his arms quietly at his side, looking down at the writhing form of the man who, a few seconds earlier, had threatened to slice him into small pieces.

Few of the men working in the supply yard had seen the brief encounter between Ki and the teamster. Their attention had been caught by the smashing of the freightwagon into the front of the saloon, and they were just now dropping whatever work they'd been doing and running to the scene of the crash. Ki glanced at the man on the ground, decided that he would be unable to stand for the next few minutes, and after kicking the knife out of reach of his defeated assailant, he walked over to the stagecoach.

Jessie and Bobby, shaken and tossed inside the careening vehicle, were just getting out of the coach. The driver still sat in his seat, a look of dazed surprise on his face. Jessie raised her eyebrows in an unspoken question.

"Yes," Ki said simply. "It's started."

"I was sure it had, when I saw that teamster deliberately trying to wreck us," she said. "You didn't take the time to ask him any questions, I noticed."

"No. It'll be a few minutes before he feels like talking,

31

and I wanted to be sure you were all right."

"A little shaken, but nothing more," Jessie said. "Bobby, how about you?"

"I'm fine, Miss Jessie," Bobby replied. "Do you really think that man was trying to hurt us? That it wasn't just an accident?"

"I'm afraid so, Bobby," Jessie said. "I haven't told you everything that's involved in this situation you and your grandfather have gotten into. I wanted to wait until we got to the valley. Would you mind if I don't explain until then?"

"No. I guess not, Miss Jessie. But if it wasn't an accident, how'd he know we was going to be on the stage?"

Ki answered him before Jessie could speak. "Word travels fast on a telegraph, Bobby. And there's only one stage running into Hidden Valley. But Jessie and your grandfather will explain everything to you. Right now we've got to do something about that man who tried to wreck us."

"What do you think we should do, Ki?" Jessie asked. "I've been thinking about him myself."

Ki shrugged. "I'm sure he won't have anything to say, when we do question him."

"Let's take him to the construction office, then," Jessie suggested. "Though I don't imagine for a minute that the South Sierra Railway superintendent will be any more helpful than your friend here."

Leaving Bobby at the stage, Jessie and Ki walked over to the teamster. He was sitting up now, rubbing his face with one hand, his other arm dangling and useless.

"All right," Ki said harshly. "Get on your feet. We're going to see what your boss has to say about what you tried to do to us a minute ago."

"I didn't do a damn thing!" the teamster snarled. "You can't go blaming a man because his team runs away!"

"You tried to kill us," Jessie said coldly. "And they put men like you in jail for attempted murder."

"You'll have to prove it!" the man replied. "And there ain't no way you'll be able to do that!"

32

Ki picked up the knife that he'd kicked aside. "We'll talk to your boss first. Now march! And don't try to run, or I'll give you a chance to feel how sharp this blade really is!"

Chapter 4

Both Jessie and Ki found that their predictions had been correct. The superintendent of the construction job listened without trying to hide his lack of interest as they described the deliberate attempt to wreck the stagecoach. When they'd finished, he looked at the teamster for a moment and shook his head.

"I never saw this man before," he said coolly. "I hope you understand that the South Sierra Railway doesn't hire teamsters. We've contracted the hauling work to a firm in San Francisco."

"If that's the case, you're not responsible for any accidents they cause, are you?" Ki asked. The tone of his voice was so gentle that it was almost sarcastic, but he looked guilelessly at the superintendent as he asked the question.

Ignoring Ki, the superintendent said to Jessie, "As I understand your story, Miss Starbuck, you and your companions in the stagecoach weren't actually in an accident.

34

I don't deny there was an accident, you understand, but it occurred across the road when the freightwagon hit the saloon, and took place after the wagon had already passed by the stage without touching it."

"Technically he's right, Ki," Jessie said quickly.

"I'm glad you agree, Miss Starbuck," the man said. "Now I suggest that you overlook the dispute this teamster had with your man. Leave this for me to settle. I'll see that the company the man works for disciplines him and pays for the damages to the saloon building."

Ki frowned and began, "Just a moment—"

Jessie broke in quickly, "Never mind, Ki. Come along. I'm sure the best thing we can do is to leave the teamster here and let the superintendent and the contractor handle things."

Walking back to the stagecoach, Ki asked Jessie, "Why were you in such a hurry to get away, Jessie? I'd like to have argued with that superintendent a little bit."

"We'd have gotten nowhere, Ki. You could see by the way he acted that he knew the accident had been planned, and he had all the answers ready."

"He was glib enough," Ki agreed. "And I'm sure he was telling the truth when he said the freighting was contracted by the railroad to another company, but I'm equally sure the other company's also one controlled by the cartel."

"Yes, of course." Jessie was silent while they walked a few steps, and then she said, "Not that we had any doubts, but this proves the cartel is behind the railroad, Ki."

"Did we really need any proof?"

Jessie shook her head. "No. But this shows us that what we've got to do now is strike them before they can get ready to attack us again, and keep on hitting them until we win!"

For the first three miles after the stagecoach left the supply depot, rails had been laid roughly parallel to the road. At the point where the completed trackage ended, a half-dozen handcars were lined up, and beyond them, crews were at

35

work setting rails. The clang of sledgehammers driving spikes into the tie-plates that held the rails firmly on the crossties filled the air as the stage rolled past the work gangs. At the points where rail lengths butted together, other gangs worked on their knees, installing fishplates to hold the joints tight.

After the rails ended, there was still another mile where pick-and-shovel crews were placing ties in gravel ballast and leveling them in line with stakes driven earlier by surveyors. When the stage passed the last of the tie-laying gangs, there was nothing but graded roadbed for several miles, with ties lying beside the grade, waiting for the crews to reach them.

"I'd say we've seen the last of the South Sierra Railway for a while," Ki commented as he looked at the wide swath the grading crews had cut across the rising terrain. "The south pass into Hidden Valley isn't too far ahead, is it, Bobby?"

"Only about another mile and a half," Bobby replied. "Mr. Abel's ranch starts just a little bit this side of the pass."

"A cattle ranch?" Jessie asked.

"Oh, sure, Miss Jessie. There's four more in the south end of the valley, too."

"Is there enough range and water in the valley to support five ranches?"

"Well, they ain't anywheres near as big as yours, but all of 'em raise cattle."

"Longhorns? Or mixed breeds?"

"Herefords, mostly. I worked on Mr. Abel's ranch during roundup. I guess maybe that's what I want to do when I grow up, is be a cowboy."

"If you do, and you ever need a job, there'll always be a place for you on the Circle Star," Jessie told him.

"I'd sure like that," Bobby said. "Mr. Wright and all the rest of 'em were real nice to me while I was there."

Ahead, the road curved sharply up a gentle rise, and shelving rock formations began to show, their sharp edges outlined in crisp detail by the westering sun. The dark strip of turned dirt that marked the railroad right-of-way ended abruptly at the beginning of the curve. The stagecoach slowed, and the shouts of the driver grew louder and came more often as he geed the team up the increasingly steep grade.

At the top of the incline the driver pulled up and called, "I got to stop here and breathe the team, if you wanta get out and stretch your legs a minute or so."

Ki swung out of the coach and lowered the stirrup-step for Jessie. She had just stepped to the ground when a man's voice behind them said politely, "Would you folks mind turning around so I can get a good look at you?"

Jessie and Ki turned to face the speaker. He was a tall, suntanned man, dressed in rancher's cords. A rifle was cradled in his elbow and Ki noticed that though the weapon was held with apparent casualness, the man had his right hand wrapped around the stock's throat and his finger was positioned to slide quickly to the trigger. Behind them, Bobby spoke from the open door of the stagecoach.

"It's all right, Clegg," the youth said. "This is Miss Starbuck and Ki. You don't need to worry about them, they've come to help Grandpa."

"Bobby Tinker!" the man with the rifle exclaimed. "Doggone you, boy! Don't you know the Captain's been fretting ever since you left? What got into you, anyhow?"

Jessie spoke quickly. "That's a long story, Mr. Clegg. Perhaps you'd better wait and let Captain Tinker tell you the details after he's talked with Bobby."

"Clegg's my first name, Miss Starbuck. Clegg Sanford. I'm Blaine Abel's ranch foreman, and I guess like everybody else in the cattle business, I've heard about you and your daddy."

"My father's dead, Mr. Sanford. And this is Ki, who— well, Ki helps me whenever I need help."

Sanford nodded to Ki, who returned the salutation. Then

37

he said to Jessie, "I'd feel better if you'd just call me Clegg, Miss Starbuck. And I'm sorry about your daddy. I know the Captain will be too."

"Father's been dead for some time, Clegg," Jessie replied. "I was surprised when Bobby told me that Captain Tinker hadn't gotten word of his death."

"We're sorta tucked away in a corner here in Hidden Valley, Miss Starbuck. It takes a long time for news to get to us."

Ki said, "I've been wondering why you met the stage with a rifle, Clegg. Has the railroad crowd been stirring up trouble?"

"Not any more'n usual."

"That could mean almost anything," Jessie said.

"Well, it means we've had some water holes salted and some steers shot at night. But it's been little piddling stuff, so far. Then, when they got the grade up to the pass a few days ago, Blaine figured they might try some kinda tricks, like setting off a charge of dynamite to open it up."

Ki nodded. "So you're guarding it. I hope you've got enough men to keep someone on duty day and night."

"Oh, Blaine's worked things out with the other ranchers. We take turns, and the work gets done, and nobody's put out much."

"From what you've said, I get the idea the ranchers aren't anxious to have a railroad through the valley," Jessie said.

"We'd *like* to have a railroad. It'd save driving steers to the Southern Pacific shipping pens up north when we take 'em to market," Clegg replied. "But not this railroad. They started out acting like crooks, and that gave us a pretty good idea how they'd act if they got in."

Before Jessie could ask Clegg any more questions, the stage driver called, "Horses are rested now. Better get moving, if we're going to make it the rest of the way before dark."

Hidden Valley, as Jessie viewed it from the stagecoach in the late afternoon sunlight, was as different from her

38

beloved Circle Star as any place could be. The valley might have been on another planet, an older and more settled world than the one on which the ranch was located. The only feature common to the two areas was that both were virtually treeless. In all other ways, Hidden Valley contrasted sharply with the endlessly sprawling, bare and unpeopled expanse of the vast southwest Texas prairie. Still, Jessie found herself drawn to the isolated pocket of green that nestled between the mountains.

For the first two or three miles, lush pastures stretched from the road on both sides. Late as the summer was, the grass in the fields was still green, and came midway up the stumpy legs of the whitefaced Hereford steers that grazed in small herds on the unfenced land. Only two of the ranch houses were visible from the road, but Bobby pointed out the locations of those that were nestled in valleys or behind low rises of the ground.

Gradually the pastures gave way to farms, where there were neat dwellings and oversized barns spaced widely apart, with fenced crop rows stretching away from them in neatly spaced lines. Most of the farm crops had been harvested, but men were working in some of the fields visible from the stagecoach. Between the bare acres where the harvest had been made and the fields freshly plowed, a few fields still showed green squares of rectangles of unpicked vegetables not yet ready to go to market.

Twilight was approaching and the sky had turned a deep, clear blue by the time the stage stopped in the town, which bore the same name as that of the valley. The driver pulled the team to a creaking halt in front of the livery stable. For a moment after they alighted, Jessie, Ki, and Bobby stood by the coach, adjusting to the lack of motion after the swaying of the top-heavy vehicle. Then, while waiting for the driver to get their luggage from the boot, they stepped out into the road to look at the town.

There were no houses near the livery stable; it was isolated by an expanse of corrals and barns from the nearest

39

dwellings. A hundred yards or so beyond the corral, the unpaved road became a street, and the town began. Ki took the two heavy bags, and Bobby carried Jessie's second piece of baggage, a light portmanteau.

They started up the street, passing two or three houses on either side, all of them well back from the road, and reached the beginning of a board sidewalk. The first buildings beyond the few set-back houses were an unusually large sprawling structure that rambled back from the sidewalk and just beyond it a tall, square frame building of two and a half stories.

As they got closer, they could see at the eaves of the high house a sign that said ROOMS. Above the narrow veranda of the first structure, an even larger sign extending to the street read SALOON. On the saloon's narrow veranda, a half-dozen men lounged on benches.

"Grandpa's house is a little ways off," Bobby told his companions. "We've got to go through town, to the other side of the courthouse square." They were approaching the saloon, and the boy added, "We can cross to the other side of the street if you don't want to walk in front of the saloon, Miss Jessie."

"Why, I don't mind one bit walking past the saloon, Bobby," Jessie smiled. "But you know where we're going. Ki and I don't, so you lead the way and we'll just follow you."

After Jessie's reassurance, Bobby chose not to cross the street. The wooden sidewalk was far too narrow to allow them to walk three abreast, and was really not wide enough for two, so Bobby led the way, a half-step ahead of Jessie, and Ki kept a step behind. As they neared the saloon, two of the half-dozen men who were on the shallow veranda moved close to the edge and eyed the walking trio. Both of the men had on Montana-creased hats, and wore neckerchiefs at the throats of their checked gingham shirts, and duck jeans tucked into high-heeled boots. Both had on pistol belts. Their attention was focused on Jessie, and she kept her eyes straight ahead, ignoring their stares.

One of the pair, a big man who towered half a head over his companion, nudged the other and said loudly, "Well, would you look there, Slip! Seems we got a new family come to town!"

"Yep, sure seems like," the man addressed as Slip replied. "I tell you, Jug, I wouldn't give much for the runt in front and the skinny fellow behind, but the one in between, I'd take home myself!"

Jessie gave no indication that she heard the exchange. The men were obviously drunk, and Jessie had learned that to pay any attention to drunken rowdies only encouraged them. For his part, Ki had long since learned to ignore such jibes. The man named Jug was not to be discouraged by being ignored, however.

"I might not let you take her, Slip," he said. "I think I could do better for her than you could."

"Well, either one of us'd be a step up from either of the two that's walking with her," Slip commented.

"Now that's the truth," Jug guffawed. "Well, I'll tell you what, Slip. I'll toss you for her."

"Yeah, you're right, Jug. You or me, either one, could chew him up and spit him out and never know we'd did it."

Jessie had seen Bobby's back stiffen when the big man made his first remark. They had reached the corner of the veranda now, and Jessie put her hand on Bobby's shoulder, hoping the boy would understand her gesture as a warning to pass on by without appearing to notice the rowdies.

Jug said to his companion, "You know, now I see her closer, I got a good mind to see if she'd like to have a real man for a change. That little piddling fellow that acts like her husband sure don't look to be man enough for a woman like her."

Bobby, Jessie, and Ki were in front of the men now.

41

Slip pointed at Ki and said, "Well, by God! Look at him, Jug! He's a damn chink!"

"Now she's way too good-lookin' to be wasted on a piece of yellow-skin trash," Jug replied. "Let's just see if she don't feel the same way."

Giving a hitch to his pistol belt, Jug stepped off the veranda to the sidewalk. He pushed Bobby into the street and planted himself in front of Jessie. Her head barely reached the big man's shoulder. She looked at him with cold eyes, and for a moment the drunken rowdy hesitated.

On the veranda, Slip guffawed, "What's wrong, Jug? Cat got your tongue? Or is your belly yellow, too?"

His companion's words gave Jug the impetus he needed. He extended his hand, reaching for Jessie's shoulder, and began, "Look here, little lady, you—"

Jessie had not attained Ki's skill in hand-to-hand combat, but her work with him had given her more than enough ability to handle a clumsy hulk like Jug. He was not prepared for the quickness with which Jessie acted. Her hands darted forward with the speed and accuracy of striking snakes. With her left hand she grasped Jug's hamlike hand, her strong fingers digging into the base of his thumb, her thumb pressing hard on the back of his hand to spread his palm. At the same time she wrapped her fingers around Jug's wrist, yanked his arm forward, then twisted his wrist down while she shoved his elbow into his bulging belly.

When he saw that his companion was in trouble, Slip stepped off the veranda, his right hand moving by habit to the butt of his holstered revolver. At Jug's first movement, Ki had dropped the suitcase he was carrying. Now he slid his left forearm into the crook of Slip's elbow, and locked his right hand around the wrist of the hoodlum's bent arm. Ki twisted Slip's wrist to bring the rowdy's hand palm-upward, then, using his own muscular forearm as a lever, he snapped the wrist down. Ki's quick, expert pressure dislocated the man's elbow. With the gargled scream of a wounded animal, Slip went to his knees, cradling his elbow

42

in his left hand. Ki slid the thug's revolver from its holster and tossed the weapon onto the shed roof that extended above the veranda.

Jug grunted with surprise as Jessie's fingertips bit into the senstive muscles bunched in the base of his thumb. The yipping turned into a yowl of pain as she pulled his forearm down, gaining leverage by pushing harder on the elbow pressing into his midsection. He tried to pull away, but his biceps were useless with his arm locked in the downward twist, and when he tried to wrest free, the tortured nerves in his hand sent shooting pains up his arm and shoulder.

Jessie maintained the hold in a static position for only a few seconds. She yanked Jug's wrist with a downward twist that sent fresh pain up his arm as both his elbow and the socket of his shoulder were strained into a position that hurt him past enduring. The hulking rowdy dropped to his knees on the sidewalk. Jessie released her hold, stepped around Jug, and moved past him to the street where Bobby stood, his mouth open, gaping at the kneeling, moaning rowdies.

Ki took Jug's pistol from its holster; the big man was too absorbed in his own pain to notice what was happening. Ki threw the gun on the roof where he'd already tossed Slip's weapon. He picked up the suitcases and nodded to Jessie. She pressed her hand on Bobby's shoulder, and the three resumed their interrupted walk to the center of town. The entire encounter had occurred so quickly that the other men on the veranda were still sitting on the benches where they'd been lounging, staring at the backs of Jessie, Ki, and Bobby as they walked leisurely along the street in the growing dusk.

★

Chapter 5

Bobby walked as silently as Jessie and Ki for a half-dozen yards, then his curiosity bubbled over. "How'd you and Ki do what you just did, Miss Jessie? Why, you took care of those two men before they knew what hit 'em! And they both had guns!"

"A gun is only as good as the reflexes of the man carrying it, Bobby," Ki said. "Jessie and I just moved faster than they did."

"Well, it sure was something to see!" the youth exclaimed. "Could you show me those holds you used, Ki?"

"Of course. But the holds are only good if your entire body is trained, and your mind prepared."

"Just the same, I'd like to know how to use them, Ki. They sure give a fellow an edge in a fight!"

"There'll be time for Ki to show you, Bobby," Jessie said. She looked up the street. "Is your grandfather's house very far from here?"

"No, ma'am. Just a little way. We're almost to the town square, and grandpa's house is just on the other side of it."

The town of Hidden Valley reminded her of some of the old villages in the New England states she'd visited. It was a neat town, but not a large one, and in the part of it Jessie and Ki saw as they followed Bobby, there were no signs that it was growing. None of the houses they passed were new. They were spaced widely apart from one another, surrounded by lawns and flowerbeds.

When they reached the square, Jessie was again reminded of New England. An uncompromisingly rectangular two-story brick building stood isolated in an area of green lawn and bore a sign above its double doors that said it was the town courthouse. A brick walk led to the entrance, the walk circling around a low, grassy mound on which a small brass cannon stood, a pyramid of cannonballs beside it.

Bobby pointed to the cannon. "I guess you've heard about General John C. Fremont, Miss Jessie? That's his cannon."

"Of course I've heard of him. He was almost elected President once. But how did the cannon get to Hidden Valley? I don't remember General Fremont fighting any battles near here."

"He wasn't coming here at all, Miss Jessie. He was leading his men over the mountains in winter, and they left the cannon up there when a storm caught them. A miner found it, and—well, I don't exactly know how it got here."

"That's very interesting," Jessie said absently. She was looking around the square. Four stores and a bank stood with vacant lots between them on two of four streets that bordered the courthouse. All of the stores were closed, and except for the loungers on the saloon veranda, she'd seen no one on the street.

Puzzled by the absence of activity, Jessie asked Bobby, "Aren't there any people in Hidden Valley except those loafers in front of the saloon?"

"Why, it's suppertime, Miss Jessie," Bobby replied. "Folks will be coming out again after while."

"And they'll stay up as late as eight or nine o'clock, I'll bet," Ki said with a smile.

"Some of them will. And there'll be some men in the saloon until real late." Bobby turned at the corner they'd reached while he was talking. He led them past two houses and up the brick walkway and onto the porch of the third. Without knocking, he opened the door and said, "Go on in, Miss Jessie."

Jessie started to enter the hallway beyond the door just as an aproned woman appeared at the other end of the passage. She saw Jessie and gave a small startled cry, then said sharply, "I was taught to knock at a stranger's door before—"

"Ma!" Bobby shouted.

"Bobby? Is it—oh, yes! Yes, it is!" Turning aside, she called, "Father! Hurry, Father! Bobby's come home!"

Bobby had already raced past Jessie down the hall and into his mother's embrace. A tall, white-haired man with a short, square-cut beard and brilliant eyes of startlingly deep sapphire blue limped into the hallway behind the pair. Bobby saw him and answered the old man's shout of welcome with a loud yell, as he exchanged his mother's embrace for the Captain's. Jessie and Ki stayed outside the door, watching silently, hesitant to intrude on the Tinkers' family reunion.

Bobby's mother left the boy with his grandfather and came to the door. "You'd be Miss Starbuck, and I'm Martha Tinker. Bobby forgot his manners, he's so excited. Do come in, please."

"Thank you. This is Ki, Mrs. Tinker. Both of us feel we know you and the Captain, Bobby's talked about you so much."

Seeing Jessie and Ki move into the hall, Bobby remembered them at last. "Grandpa," he said, taking Captain Tinker's hand and pulling him toward them, "this is Miss Jessie Starbuck and this is Ki. They came with me all the way from Texas."

Captain Tinker smiled and extended his hand to Jessie.

46

"I can't find the words to say how pleased I am to see you at last, Miss Starbuck, and I thank you for taking care of Bobby as you did. He shouldn't have run away in the first place, but Martha and I are so glad to see him back that we've agreed to overlook that."

"I'm just glad we were at the ranch when he got there," Jessie said. "There are times when we're away for weeks."

"It's all worked out well, I'd say," Tinker replied. He was talking to Jessie, but she saw his eyes focused beyond her, on the front door. He went on, "Anyhow, I thank you as much as Martha does for bringing Bobby back to us, safe and sound." Taking his eyes from the door at last, he asked Jessie with a worried frown, "I guess Alex couldn't come with you?"

Jessie replied softly, "Father's dead, Captain Tinker. I should have mentioned that in the telegram I sent telling you that Bobby was safe and I'd see that he got home. It just didn't occur to me that you might not know. But I'm sure he'd be here too, if he were still alive."

Her words seemed to stun the old man. He swallowed hard and his brilliant blue eyes grew misty. For a moment, Jessie could see him transported almost physically through years of memories to a past when he and a young Alex Starbuck had shared adventures of which she knew little or nothing. The moment passed, and Tinker looked at her and shook his head.

"No. I didn't know," he said. His voice was a bit unsteady at first, but it grew stronger as he spoke. "Alex being so much younger than me, I thought I'd go first. But after I left the sea and settled here, with a lot of help from Alex, he got so busy with all his businesses and things that I didn't see him as often as I did in the days when we—" He saw the effect his words were having on Jessie, and stopped short. "I'm sorry, Jessie. This isn't the time for us to talk about your father."

"We'll find time later," Jessie promised.

"Yes, of course. And I'm not a good host, or we'd be

in the parlor now, or in the dining room, if you haven't had supper."

"We haven't, Grandpa," Bobby broke in. "And I'm hungry."

Belatedly, Jessie remembered Ki. She took his hand and pulled him up beside her and said, "Ki was Alex's helper and friend for a long time, Captain Tinker. He's now helping me and being the same kind of friend he was to Alex."

"Ki! Of course!" Tinker took Ki's hand in both of his. "I know from Alex's last letters how much he thought of you, Ki. And if—" He hesitated momentarily, then went on, "Well, I met your mother, and I knew your father well. We'll have to talk, too."

Ki had listened to the brief exchange between Jessie and the Captain, and having seen the effect resurgent memories had on her, he was holding his own feelings in firm control. He returned the pressure of Tinker's gnarled but strong hands and said, "We'll talk, Captain. There will be time."

"Of course there will."

Martha Tinker said to Jessie, "I know you're tired after such a trip. Now if you and Ki will come along with me, I'll show you your rooms, and you can freshen up while I set places at the supper table for you. I'm sure you haven't had a decent meal since you started up here on the stage. The Captain and I were just sitting down to supper when you got here, and there's plenty for all of us."

Jessie and Ki had been happy enough to let Bobby monopolize the conversation at the table. They had put in an occasional word, but for the most part were listeners. With dinner behind them, Martha had shooed the others into the parlor, waving aside Jessie's offer and another from Ki to help wash the dishes.

"I'm never at home in a strange kitchen, and I know nobody else is," she'd said. "Bobby usually helps me, but I'll let him off tonight, because I know he's tired, and he's

48

going to bed right now." She gave Bobby a look that fore-
stalled any protest and went on, "Captain, you and Jessie
and Ki can do your talking in the parlor. Now. all of you
clear out and don't argue with me!"

As they found chairs in the parlor, the Captain said, "You
know, Jessie, when I was younger, I'd have been able to
handle a thing like this, but a man slows down when he
gets to be my age."

"Has there been trouble, then?" Jessie asked.

"A bit. Not as much as I'd feared. But things have been
happening that I don't like." Tinker was tamping tobacco
into a stubby-stemmed briar pipe as he spoke. "I don't need
to tell you and Ki how the cartel does its dirty work, Jessie,
and I've seen enough of that outfit at work to know its ways.
I'll tell you this to begin with: the cartel's almost ready to
start its dirty work right here in town. You and Ki got here
just in time to give us the help we need."

"That's what we came for," Jessie said. "But we have
to know the situation before we can make any plans."

"It's bad and getting worse," Tinker told her. "I'll tell
you why Bobby heard me say so many times that I wished
your father was here, Jessie. I know that Alex had a lot of
friends back east in Washington, and I hoped he could get
some soldiers or militia or something sent here to protect
us."

Jessie was silent for a moment while she tried to think
of a way to explain to the old seaman why his hope was
futile. She said, "I'm afraid nobody could do that, Captain.
The Starbuck name still means a lot in Washington, but the
cartel's worked men into the government, too. If you play
chess, you'll know what 'stalemate' means."

Tinker grinned crookedly. "It's what you'd call a Mex-
ican standoff, I guess. Nobody loses, nobody wins."

Jessie nodded. "That's close enough. The federal officials controlled by the cartel can stop us, the ones who owe
us favors can stop the cartel, but neither of us has enough

49

strength to win over the other. And the cartel's good at keeping its activities hushed up, so we can't even count on public indignation to help our cause."

Ki said thoughtfully. "You should have enough war veterans in the valley to form a pretty good fighting force, though."

Captain Tinker shook his head. "There's not all that many, Ki. And it was a bitter war they fought in. The old grudges still hang on. Whether they wore a blue uniform or a gray one, no man wants to stand shoulder to shoulder with one who fought on the other side. Besides, they've all had a bellyful of fighting."

"And you can't persuade them?" Jessie asked.

"They don't listen to me anymore, Jessie," Tinker said sadly. "I try to tell 'em the railroad bunch won't wait for us to get organized. They're already pushing us. I guess you saw how the railroad's graded right up to the south pass now."

Ki nodded. "Yes, we saw that. But your guards should be able to keep them from taking the pass."

"We met the guard there when the stage stopped," Jessie explained. "He told us what the ranchers are doing."

"That's Blaine Abel's idea," Tinker said. "At least he's doing something. But one man can't do it all, Jessie."

"I understood all the ranchers are helping," she frowned.

"They are. And that makes five men." The Capatin shook his head. "It's not enough."

"We'll help, of course," Jessie said quickly. "But if the railroad's going to be stopped, the people who live right here in Hidden Valley will have to do it."

"So far, the ranchers in the south end of the valley are the only ones who've done anything," the Captain said. "All that the farmers and folks in town have done is talk."

"From what Bobby said, the grading work to the north hasn't gotten as close to the valley as the grade to the south," Jessie frowned. "Are they right at the pass there, too?"

"No. On the north it's still five or six miles away. But

50

the railroad's not waiting till their grade gets closer. They've got men working for them in the valley right now."

"Working?" Ki said. "How?"

"Scaring people, mostly. A man named Karl Prosser showed up here about a month ago with a big roll of cash. He said he was buying farms and houses for some land company in the East, but I smelled the railroad behind him the minute he opened his mouth."

"And it smells to me like the cartel behind the railroad," Jessie said thoughtfully. "The cartel's like an octopus, Captain. And if you cut off one of its arms, two grow in its place. But I guess you learned that from my father."

"I did, Jessie, when Alex first crossed swords with them, a long time ago."

"They've gotten bigger since then, and even more vicious. But has this Prosser been able to find many people who are willing to sell?"

"Not so far. But when his money didn't get him anywhere, he started talking mean. Now he's telling everybody that if they don't sell out, he's going to bring in lawyers and take their farms and houses away from them."

Ki asked, "Surely nobody believes such an unlikely story?"

"Some of them don't think it's all that unlikely, Ki."

"Why?"

"That's sort of my fault, I guess," Tinker frowned.

"We need to know everything you can tell us," Jessie said. "What does Prosser say he'll do to make good on his threats?"

"That goes back quite a ways," the Captain began, his voice showing his reluctance. "I wasn't in very good shape when your father gave me this valley, Jessie. My leg was giving me hell. It's gotten better over the years—"

Jessie interrupted to say, "I know about your wound, and how you got it, Captain. I have all of father's diaries. I read about the fight, and in a later diary there was an entry that Father had given you the land here."

51

"Did it say anything about a deed?"

After she'd thought for a moment, Jessie replied, "Yes, I'm sure the diary mentioned a deed. Why?"

"Because there's not any record of it at the courthouse, and unless I can prove the land was mine to sell or give away, the folks I sold it to can't lawfully claim it."

"Why, that's nonsense!" Jessie exclaimed.

"Maybe." The Captain's tone of voice showed he was not convinced. "Prosser says different. He's telling everybody that any deed I gave them is worthless unless I can prove I had the right to give it to them."

"But when land changes hands, the deed has to be recorded at the courthouse," Jessie said. "The county clerk has to check the title, to make sure it's clear. Didn't you and the people who bought land from you do that?"

"I told all of them what to do, but I didn't go to the courthouse with them and make sure they did it. I gave away a lot of land, too. There were some kinfolks who wanted to settle where we could sort of be a family again, and I had a lot more than I'd ever need, so I gave them enough for a house or farm."

"And your relatives recorded those deeds too?"

"I suppose they did. I told them to. But it's been a lot of years since I got rid of the last of the land Alex gave me, and the new county clerk says he can't find any records that the deeds were ever filed."

Ki said, "It smells to me like the cartel began buying the county officials even before they broke the news about the railroad being built."

"You may be right, Ki," the Captain agreed. "It's been my experience that people will do almost anything if they get paid enough to make it worth their while."

"But you can give them another deed now," Jessie suggested. "I'm sure there's no law against that."

"Except that I've got to prove I owned the land to begin with," Tinker reminded her.

"Well, that's not going to be hard to do," Jessie told him

52

cheerfully. "Somewhere there's certainly an official record that my father owned this land, and if your original deed was lost, I can give you one, as his heir."

"Jessie, I've learned something about these folks here in Hidden Valley," Tinker said. "Most of them never owned any land before, and there's not many of them ever had anything to do with the law. Well, take me. I know sea law, but it's simple and easy to understand, because there's not any lawyers on a ship to mix folks up with fancy language that nobody but another lawyer can figure out."

"Perhaps I can help you make the Hidden Valley people understand things like land deeds and transfers," Jessie suggested.

"I imagine you can," the old man told her. "Like I just told you, they're tired of listening to me. Even some of my kinfolks think I'm just a bossy old codger. But a minute ago you said something about the cartel being like an octopus. Their other arms have been busy too. They're not depending on using just the law in this fight."

"You mean they're planning to force the passes?" Ki asked.

"They might be, Ki. I can't say for sure," Tinker replied. "It's the town I've got in mind. I could tell from the way you hushed up Bobby at the table that he didn't tell all there was to know about that fracas you had at the saloon on the way here."

"That was just a brush with a couple of drunken rowdies," Jessie said. "There were more pleasant things to talk about during dinner."

"I'll grant you that. But I'm concerned about what's been going on at that saloon."

"Why? It's not any different from any other saloon, is it?"

"It was better than most until a few weeks ago," the Captain said. "Old John Litzman owned it before that. Everybody called him Dutch John. He was one of the first ones to come to the valley, and he was a good man, ran a

53

nice, clean, orderly saloon where you could go in for a drink or two and meet your friends and talk." Tinker shook his head sadly. "It's not like that anymore."

"You mean Litzman's changed?" Jessie asked.

"He sold out. Didn't say a word to anybody, just up anchor and left, overnight."

"Didn't he tell anyone he was selling out?"

"Not even me, and I sold him the land he built the place on, when the town was just a pup."

"Are you sure the cartel bought it?"

"Look at it from their side, Jessie," Tinker said. "They'd need a headquarters in town here. Where could they find one that suited them better?"

"But you're not sure?"

"If I was still a gambling man, like I was when I was young, I'd lay you any amount you'd care to put up that they either offered Dutch John so much money that he couldn't turn it down, or they threatened to kill him if he didn't sell to them."

Jessie said, "And all the changes have taken place since the new owners took the place over?"

"They sure have," Tinker said emphatically. He tugged at his beard thoughtfully, then went on, "You know, Jessie, I used to to be a pretty good rounder when I was a young fellow, just going to sea. I've been in all kinds of waterfront dives in most any port you'd care to name, and I can smell a bad one and a crooked one the minute I push through the batwings."

"Yes. I'd imagine you've seen just about all kinds," Jessie agreed. "And Dutch John's is a bad one now?"

"It's got the smell, just in the short time since he left. Dutch never allowed a woman through his door, never had a card game going, and he'd close down about ten o'clock at night. But as soon as the woman took charge of the place, all that changed."

"A woman's running the saloon?" Ki asked.

"She sure is." The Captain snorted, a mixture of anger

and disgust. "I guess her name's Cherry, only she's French-ified it and calls herself Cheri." He exaggerated the pronunciation, stressing the accent on the second syllable.

"I get the idea that the changes she's made weren't for the better," Ki went on.

Tinker snorted again. "Better! The place is full of the kind of riffraff that gave you trouble. Most of them are plug-uglies from God knows where. And that Cherry's brought in floozies and gambling layouts and she keeps the place open around the clock."

"Well, Jessie," Ki said, "it looks like we've each got a job to do. You can work with the Captain and try to find out what's going on at the courthouse, and I'll spend my time at the saloon and see what I can learn there."

"That could be dangerous, Ki," Tinker said. "Those two men you had that run-in with are sure to recognize you."

"I can look after myself, Captain. Don't worry."

"Well, if you don't mind walking into a lion's cage, it'll keep you busy while Jessie's helping me get the mess about the land titles unraveled," Tinker said thoughtfully. He looked at Jessie. "You've had a long, hard trip, all the way from Texas. I imagine you'll want to rest up a few days?"

Jessie and Ki exchanged smiles, and Jessie said, "Ki and I are used to traveling, Captain. The sooner we start, the sooner we'll overcome the lead the cartel seems to have on us. If it's all right with you, let's begin tomorrow."

★

Chapter 6

Jessie had not expected to have a red carpet rolled out by the county officials when she and Captain Tinker told them what they'd come to do, but she hadn't expected the almost open hostility they encountered.

Zeke Carter, the wizened little county clerk, stared at them with almost colorless blue eyes when he heard their request to examine the land deeds.

"You tell me what deed you wanta look at," he said. "I'll get it for you."

"You don't seem to understand, Zeke," the Captain told the man. "We want to look at all the deeds you've got on file."

"I never heard of such a thing! I can't have outsiders messing up my files and books!" Carter protested.

"I guess I better go see Judge Halstead, then," Tinker told the clerk. "He'll read the law to you."

"You can't," Zeke smirked. "The judge is in San Francisco. He won't be back for another week or two."

A chair scraped in the room across the hall, and a pudgy man with a sheriff's badge pinned on his blue shirt appeared in the doorway. He looked at Jessie and Tinker, and asked the clerk, "You having trouble, Zeke?"

"Oh, Cap'n Bob and this lady wanta look at some deeds, and I been trying to tell 'em why they can't," Carter whined.

"You say the word," the sheriff began, "and I'll—"

"You'll do nothing, Ed Kinsell!" Tinker snapped. "You know the law about public records, and we do too! They're open to any taxpayer who wants to look at them!"

Kinsell hesitated a moment, then told Carter, "I guess you got to let 'em look, Zeke. Cap'n Bob's right."

Carter nodded slowly. "All right," he told the Captain. "You can look at the books up here. We ain't got room to keep everything in the little office, though. The deeds are stored down in the basement."

Ki saw Captain Tinker's buggy in front of the courthouse as he crossed the square. He thought of Jessie, who must now be digging into dusty records in some storage room and felt a touch of sympathy for her. Then, as he walked on and saw the saloon ahead, Ki wondered if his sympathy might not be better saved for himself.

Today there were no loungers in front of the saloon, and when Ki pushed through the batwings he was surprised to see that the place was empty. Except for an aproned barkeep who stood with his back to the cavernous room, polishing glasses at the backbar, Ki was the saloon's only occupant.

For a moment the barkeep watched Ki in the backbar mirror, and a puzzled frown formed on his face, growing deeper as the man's eyes studied Ki's loose blouse, worn black leather vest, unpressed trousers, and black cotton slippers with rope soles. Ki suppressed the smile that twitched his lips. The barkeep was not the first to be baffled by Ki's unorthodox clothing.

57

Unhurriedly, the man finished wiping the glass, placed it on the backbar shelf, and stepped up to the bar. When he turned to face Ki directly for the first time, his eyes grew wide.

Before the barkeep could speak, Ki put a cartwheel on the bar and said, "Beer, please. And draw one for yourself."

"Thanks just the same. I got a long night ahead, but if you're in a treating mood, I'll have a cigar."

Ki nodded, and watched the barkeep inspecting him in the backbar mirror while he filled a big-footed glass stein at the beer taps. He took a cigar from one of the boxes above the till and held it for Ki to see, then tucked it in his vest pocket.

"I'll smoke it later, I just finished one," the barkeep said, wiping the bottom of the heavy stein on his apron before putting it on the bar in front of Ki.

Ki nodded again. He knew "later" meant that the cigar would be returned to the box and its price taken from the till and put in the man's pocket. The barkeep took the silver dollar to the till, returned, and put on the bar in front of Ki a half-dollar, a twenty-five-cent piece, a dime, and a nickel. When Ki did not pick up either the beer or the change, the man could restrain his curiosity no longer.

"Say, ain't you the one that wiped up on Jug and Slip when they tried to get fresh with your wife yesterday?" he asked.

"I punished a hooligan. But the lady is not my wife. I work for her."

"That right? Well, all anybody talked about in here last night was the Chinese fellow that put Jug down."

"I happen to be Japanese," Ki said quietly.

"Sorry, I was just telling you what they said."

"I'm not offended. Many people make the same mistake."

"Everybody was wondering how in hell you could handle Jug."

Ki shrugged and said, "It was not hard." Then, looking

for information as well as changing the subject, he asked, "Did you work here when Dutch John owned the saloon?"

"No. Cheri hired me."

"Did Cheri buy the place from Dutch John?"

"No, she just manages it. Funny, I was keeping the bar at the New Ophir in Virginia City, and Cheri was dealing faro. We knew each other, sure, but not all that good, and I was the most surprised man in the world when she got the job of running this place here. She just came up to me and said, 'Mort, I need somebody I can trust. I'll give you ten a week more than you get here if you'll come along with me.' So I did."

"Then you're not acquainted with the new owner?"

"I wouldn't know him if I saw him, don't know his name or anything about him. Why?" Mort looked pointedly at Ki's loose blouse and went on, "You ain't dressed like it, but if you're a whiskey drummer or some other kind of peddler, Cheri's the one you need to talk to. When I said she runs the place, I meant it. She might not own it, but she's the boss."

"What time does she usually get in?"

"She oughta be showing up pretty soon now. The bank closes in another hour or so, and she's got to carry last night's take down there and get the change we need for tonight."

"If you don't mind, I'll wait for her. But don't let me keep you from your work. I'll call you when I want more beer."

"You do that. Cheri'll be here pretty soon."

Mort moved down to the other end of the bar and opened the door of a closet. He loaded one of his arms with unopened bottles of whiskey and began replenishing the backbar stock. He'd worked his way well along the length of the bar, and Ki had half-emptied his glass when the back door opened and a woman came in.

She glanced only casually at Ki. From the businesslike way she moved, and the air of authority she carried, Ki was

59

as certain as though he'd been introduced that she was Cheri. He had not gotten a clear view of her face when she first came in, for she'd passed him too quickly as she went to the bar. When she turned to face the backbar mirror, and Ki could see her face, he almost gaped with surprise. Cheri's eyes were almost as almond-shaped as his own.

Ki lifted his stein to make his stare less obvious while he studied Cheri's face. The Oriental cast of her features was not as pronounced as his, and he guessed that she was either of the same mixture of Oriental and Caucasian blood as himself, or of old-line Hawaiian ancestry.

Cheri was a big woman, not fat, but generously and symmetrically proportioned. Her coloring was vivid, her features bold. She stood taller than Ki, her height emphasized by the pouf of raven-black hair that arced above her high forehead. Thin black eyebrows ran in almost straight lines above her large brown eyes. Her cheekbones were high-boned, and Ki's keen eyes could tell that their ruddiness was not from a cosmetic jar, but was natural. Her nose was out of character with her face; it was aquiline, thin, and looked a trifle overlong, tapering boldly above full, pouting lips and a firm, rounded chin.

Cheri wore a shawl, and as she stood talking with the barkeep, she shrugged to let it drape loosely down her back and show the smooth skin of her shoulders. The dress that was revealed when the shawl fell away was cut fashionably low, its neckline swooping in a semicircle to display the twin swells of bulging breasts and the rosy vee between them. Ki tried to guess how old she was, but could not; with her tautly smooth skin, she could have been any age from her mid-twenties to her late thirties.

Cheri's talk with Mort was brief, and Ki was sure the barkeep had told her of his questions, for several times her eyes flicked quickly over him in the mirror. After a few moments, Cheri nodded briskly and started toward Ki's end of the bar, Mort following her on the other side of the mahogany.

Ki had used his beer glass as a shield for his observation, holding it tilted to his mouth while he kept his eyes on the mirror, and it was empty except for a film of clinging suds. He set it down. Both the barkeep and Cheri stopped just before they reached Ki. Mort opened the drawer of the till, took out a canvas sack, and handed it to her. She turned to face Ki.

"I'm Cheri," she said. Her voice gave Ki no clue to her origin. It was full and deep, a rich contralto.

"My name is Ki."

"Mort says you want to talk to me."

"If you can spare the time," Ki replied.

"I can't right now, I've got to get to the bank. If you'd like to wait for me, I'll be back in about five minutes."

"I'm not in any hurry. I'll be glad to wait."

"You might as well have a beer on the house while you're waiting," Cheri said. As she started for the door, she called to the barkeep, "Mort, draw one for Ki."

Mort took Ki's stein to the tap and refilled it. When he brought it back and set it in front of Ki, he said, "Cheri's as curious as everybody else about how you put Jug down. I told her you wasn't trying to sell her something. Hope I was right."

"You were." Ki sipped from his stein.

"Are you going to tell Cheri?"

"Tell her what?"

"How you was able to put Jug down yesterday."

"Why are you so curious about that, Mort?"

"Because Jug's a hell of a big man, and you're pretty skinny, no offense intended."

"I'm not offended. And I used a wrestling hold on Jug, there's no secret about it."

"Well, you put him out of commission for a while. And the lady hurt Slip almost as bad."

"We did nothing to bother them. They accosted us."

"Oh, sure. Nobody but the two of them blames you."

Mort went back to his interrupted work, leaving Ki wondering whether Captain Tinker could be mistaken about the saloon having become a cartel headquarters, and whether Cheri had given the barkeep orders that Ki be made to feel secure while he waited. He was still wondering when Cheri returned. She gave Mort the canvas bag that she'd taken with her and came to where Ki sat.

Looking at him with undisguised curiosity, she said, "Now. I'm free for a little while. What did you want to talk about?"

Ki looked at Mort, then gestured to one of the tables at the opposite side of the room and said, "Suppose we sit over there?"

Cheri's eyes narrowed as she looked at Ki speculatively. She said, "If you want privacy, you won't get any in here. The place starts coming to life about this time of the day."

Ki concealed the surprise and suspicion that flashed through his mind, and decided quickly that a chance to learn more outweighed the risk. He replied, "I'm open to suggestions."

"I live next door. We can talk there without anybody coming in to interrupt us."

"That sounds like a good idea. Lead the way, I'll follow."

Ki followed Cheri to the back door by which she'd come in, and they went through it into a narrow hall where the scent of new lumber hung heavy. Small rooms, no more than ten-by-ten-foot cubicles, were being built on both sides of the wide back room, a narrow corridor between them. The work was still incomplete, and Ki examined the cubicles curiously as he followed Cheri out the back door into a narrow, bare yard enclosed by a high board fence, which was also new. Ki realized at once that he was at the back of the rooming house whose sign he'd seen from the street.

"I know what you're thinking, but you're wrong," Cheri said. "The owner says he's got a crew of workmen coming in here for a job, and he's fixing a place for them to sleep."

As he followed Cheri toward the door of the house, Ki framed a question to test her. He asked, "Suppose the owner

62

brought in women instead of men, and turned those cubbyholes into a place to work. What would you—"

Cheri did not let him finish. "I'll jump off that bridge when I come to it. I've sold drinks in a lot of saloons, but that's all I've sold. I don't do anything I can't live with, and whatever anybody else wants to do is their business."

They reached the house, and Cheri took a key from her pocket and unlocked the door. A steep, narrow stairway took them to the second floor, where Cheri unlocked a second door. Light streamed through the doorway when she opened the door. She stepped aside and motioned for Ki to go in.

What he saw made Ki gasp. The room's walls were draped with billowing folds of rosy silk, and white silk formed a canopy beneath the ceiling, from the center of which hung a crystal chandelier. A mellow blue Persian carpet covered the floor. Pillow-strewn divans faced each other at one end of the room, and easy chairs stood here and there, with low tables beside them. There were richly carved cabinets standing against two of the walls. Ki had stopped just inside the door. Cheri closed it and stepped up beside him.

"I didn't fix this place up," she said. "It goes with the job, and it was like this when I moved in. I'm still not used to it, but I'm sure learning to enjoy it." She indicated the divans, and Ki sat down on one of them. Cheri sat across from him. She went on, "Well, you wanted to talk, Ki. Go ahead."

"You haven't been here long, have you, Cheri?"

"A month or so. Mort told me you wanted to know where I came from, and now I want to know why you're interested."

Ki replied with an excuse he'd used before. "It's part of my job to find out things about people."

"For that woman you work for?" When Ki didn't reply, Cheri asked, "Why should she want to know about me?"

"When she doesn't confide in me, I don't ask questions."

"We're in the same boat, aren't we, Ki? I don't ask my boss any questions, either. I don't know him all that well. He was a regular customer at the saloon where I worked in Virginia City, and when he offered me this job, the money was too good to turn down. Not many bar girls get a chance like this, without a lot of strings being tied to it."

"And you don't have any strings?"

"None that I don't tie my own knots in. And that's what the women of my people do, tie their own knots."

Ki was already pretty sure, but he guessed, "Hawaii?"

Cheri nodded. "Maui. But I left the islands ten years ago. What about you, Ki? You're part Japanese, I can see that. What's the other part?"

"My mother was Japanese, my father American."

"That's enough for us to be some kind of half-cousins, and keep us honest with each other. What about your strings?"

"I don't have any, if you're thinking about Jessie. I work for her, like you work for your boss." Ki stood up. "And if you can't tell me anything about him, I'm going to have to find someone else who might be able to."

"You don't have to go, you know," Cheri said quietly, her eyes fixed intently on Ki.

He returned her stare with equal intensity, and asked, "Are you thinking about tying knots?"

"I told you, that's the woman's privilege among my people. A very loose knot, though Ki. And only if you're interested."

Ki's first thought was that while the knot might be a snare, there was a possibility that having Cheri tie one could prove to be to his advantage. He also trusted his ability to break any string that she might try to wind around him, and from the moment she'd walked into the saloon, he'd been fully aware of her attractions.

"I'm interested," he admitted.

"I thought you might be."

Cheri stood up. She stepped over to Ki, and for the first

time he was close enough to her to be aware of the scent of her perfume, delicate but sensuous. His eyes were drawn to the deep cleft of her breasts. Bending forward, Ki pressed his face into the warm, narrow valley. He caressed the smooth skin of her ripe bulges with his lips and tongue, and Cheri sighed softly. Ki felt her hands moving up his thighs, and the warmth of her fingers at his crotch. Her breath fanned his cheek softly.

"I like what I'm finding," she whispered. "Let's go where we can be more comfortable."

Taking his hand, Cheri led Ki to a pleat in the silken wall drapery, and pulled it aside to reveal an open door. He followed her into a room that was unlighted except for the warm, rosy glow filtering through the almost transparent silk that fell back over the doorway after they'd entered. There was enough light for Ki to see that the room's principal piece of furniture was a massive double bed.

As soon as they entered the room, Cheri's hands went to her back and she started unbuttoning her dress. The dress began to slip over the globes of her breasts. She sped its crumpling slide to the floor, and removed her pantalettes with one quick sweep of her hands down her thighs.

Ki kept his eyes fixed on Cheri as she undressed in the soft translucent light, while he untied the *surushin* he'd wrapped around his waist in place of a belt, and let his trousers and breechclout fall to the floor, then shed his black leather vest. He shook off his slippers and moved to where Cheri was standing, her lush, nude body bathed in the soft, filtered glow. The rosettes of her swelling breasts had budded in anticipation, and their dark, rosy nipples drew Ki's lips to them.

Cheri shuddered as Ki's tongue explored the firm tips, his mouth moving from one to the other. Her soft hands made a warm cradle for his erection as she pressed her hips to him and parted her thighs. Ki felt the soft rasping of her sparse pubic hair as Cheri guided him into her, then suddenly he was supporting the full weight of her body when she clasped her arms around his neck and her legs around his hips and pulled him deeply into her.

"I couldn't wait," she said, her mouth close to Ki's ear. "It's been too long since I've had a man like you inside me!"

Ki did not answer, but sought her lips. Cheri's tongue darted to seek his. As their tongues entwined sinuously, Ki clasped his hands beneath Cheri's buttocks and lifted her, then buried himself deeper in her.

Holding her suspended, Cheri's arms still enbracing him, Ki began stroking with quick, hard thrusts. Her body started quivering almost at once. She was writhing in midair, her hips jerking in a long, frantic spasm while Ki slowed his strokes and stopped them when her spasm ended and he felt her grow limp.

Cheri's lips left his with a sigh. She let her head sag and come to rest on his bare shoulder. When her gasping subsided, she whispered, "I'm sorry, Ki. I just couldn't wait. I won't be in such a hurry the next time."

Ki kissed Cheri's soft shoulder and carried her to the bed, still buried deeply in her. Lowering her gently until she lay back full length, her thighs still spread by the weight of this body, Ki pushed Cheri's knees down until they touched the bed at her sides. When he braced the soles of her feet on his chest and leaned down above her, Cheri's eyes grew wide and her mouth opened in an O of astonishment.

"You're even bigger than you were before!" she gasped. "Is what I'm feeling real, Ki?"

"Very real indeed. And so is this."

Ki raised his hips and began burying himself with a slow, measured pressure. Cheri tired to bring her hips up to meet him, but her legs were locked in place by the weight of Ki's chest on her feet. Her back arched and she started rolling her hips in a side-to-side rotation as Ki sank into her, and when he lifted his own hips and began to drive deeply in a slow, sustained rhythm, a sighing moan began flowing from her throat.

Cheri's moans grew more and more frantic as Ki continued his leisurely plunging, and the rolling of her hips became wilder as she reached a climax. Ki did not slow down while her body jerked and her cries trailed off as she peaked and passed into motionless calm. He did not slow or stop when Cheri quickly went into another writhing spasm, this one prolonged for several minutes.

"Don't stop because I'm screaming, Ki!" she urged, her words coming in panting gusts. "I can't bear what you're doing to me, but I can't stand for you to stop!"

Ki did not stop, but the ecstasy and pain that mingled in Cheri's cries as he contined thrusting were bringing him to a climax, and he had no wish to falter or stop until he could share it with Cheri.

She was thrashing beneath him by now, each moment carrying her closer to another peak. Ki tightened his control and kept driving, his eyes closed now, as were Cheri's. He felt her inner muscles beginning to tighten and grasp him, and he lunged with triphammer ferocity, his hips meeting Cheri's unturned thighs with fleshy thwacks at the end of each hard thrust. She began the high-pitched screams that marked her final moments. Ki thrust again and again until he felt Cheri's lush body heaving beneath him in her last quivering spasm.

Then Ki let go, and his hips kept thrusting of their own volition as he fell forward on the cushion of warm, soft flesh beneath him, and with a sigh of contentment he closed his eyes while his taut, driven muscles grew softly relaxed. Cheri lay quietly, her eyes closed, the snowy globes of her breasts no longer heaving. Ki saw that she'd dropped off to sleep, and he closed his eyes and slept too.

★

Chapter 7

Ki woke with a start from a short, vivid dream in which he was wading waist-deep in the warm water of the Pacific Ocean, off the sandy shore of a tropical island. As always when he awoke, he was instantly aware of where he was and what had happened last before he slept, and even before he looked at Cheri, he was smiling. She was kneeling beside his hips, bending forward, her full lips closed around his beginning erection.

Cheri straightened up, releasing him, and returned the smile. She said, "I didn't know you were such a light sleeper, Ki. You woke up so fast that I didn't have enough time to enjoy my favorite way of waking a man."

"Now that I am awake, I'll share your enjoyment."

"That may be even better."

Cheri bent forward again, and Ki felt the moist tip of her tongue flicking him as lightly as the brushing of a butterfly's wings. To avoid depriving Cheri of her enjoyment, he allowed himself to become erect very slowly indeed, and to increase her share of the pleasure, he slid his hand between her thighs, found the small, pliant button nestled between her inner lips, and rubbed it gently with the tip of a finger.

Cheri responded by lingeringly caressing his erection with the full width of her moist tongue before she took his rigid shaft entirely inside her mouth. For a few moments she held him deeply, her warm tongue slipping sinuously around, then she began bobbing her head slowly up and down.

Ki felt the button he was fingering growing firm and slickly moist. Cheri's thigh muscles began to quiver, and the rhythmic movements of her head faltered and stopped. She released him and straightened up, gazing at the glistening, moist cylinder that she had brought to life.

"I'd love to carry you all the way, Ki," she said. "Later I will. Right now I'm burning up, and all I can think about is getting you inside me again as quick as possible."

"Then do," he invited. "What pleases you most will please me as well."

Before Ki had stopped speaking, Cheri was straddling his hips and lowering herself on his erection. She shivered as his penetration deepened, and began rocking back and forth on her knees, her budded breasts quivering. Ki caressed their tips with his fingers, and Cheri arched her back and brought her body erect to press down with greater force on the impaling flesh. Sharp, small sighs, like birdcalls, formed in her throat and bubbled from her taut lips, and her body began jerking spasmodically.

"Deeper, Ki, deeper!" she cried. "You're filling me wonderfully, but I still want more!"

Ki grasped Cheri's waist in both hands and pulled her down, holding her firmly against his hips while she trembled and twisted through her orgasm. When her tremors began fading and her panting lessened, he lifted her off his still

69

rigid shaft, and with catlike quickness rolled away, leaving Cheri lying facedown on the bed.

On his feet beside the bed, Ki clamped his muscular hands on Cheri's upraised hips and went into her from behind. She cried out when his hips met her upraised buttocks at the end of his first, almost brutal penetration, but her cry was one of joy. Cheri kept screaming softly, her throaty ululations of pleasure shaded with pain, while Ki stroked faster and faster.

She went into orgasm almost at once, her body trembling in waves. Ki carried her through its tide, and when he did not stop or slow his pounding thrusts, Cheri's soft screams became frantic, mounting in intensity as Ki kept driving, controlling his own growing urge, and her cries grew to a peak as her spasm began shaking her.

In the midst of Cheri's wild bucking gyrations, Ki let loose with everything he had. He stood trembling gently, pulling Cheri's soft buttocks hard against his belly, until he had drained completely and she sagged limply on the bed. Then Ki released her, let himself fall on the bed, and stretched out beside her.

For a long while they lay silently, then Cheri whispered, "I never thought a man could give me as much as you have, Ki. I'm sorry I had to stop when I was waking you up."

"My pleasure was as great as yours. We owe each other nothing, except more pleasure later."

Propping herself on an elbow, Cheri looked down at him and shook her head. "That's not what I'm getting at. I'd like to have you stay around."

"I will, for a while. I can't say exactly how long, but—"

Cheri interrupted him. "Ki, I'm serious. What would it take to get you to quit this woman you're working for, and stay here in Hidden Valley with me?"

Ki shook his head. "What I do is much better than working in a saloon. I don't think I'd care for that."

"I wasn't thinking of the saloon," Cheri told him. "From the way you handled yourself in that fight—well, it wasn't much of a fight, from what I heard—but anyhow, you'd be worth a lot to my boss. If I told him—"

"Who is your boss, Cheri?"

"His name is Frank Jeffers. I'm afraid I really don't know much about him, except that he's got an awful lot of money. He owns mines or something in Virginia City."

"Might I have seen him around these parts?" Ki asked.

Cheri smiled. "Hell, you'd know it if you did. He's good-looking, and has the money to keep himself that way. Tall and real distinguished—gray hair and mustache, an embroidered vest, a fine pearl-gray derby hat, and a diamond stickpin. He's real fond of that stickpin, always wears it. He's a faro player. I was dealing at the New Ophir up in Virginia City, that's how I met him. He knows how to charm a lady, that's for sure." She smiled, then shrugged. "I don't guess I know much more about him than that."

"Those rooms he's having built behind the saloon," Ki said thoughtfully. "You said he was bringing a lot of men in here for some kind of work. What kind, Cheri?"

"I—I don't know. He didn't explain."

"And this house," Ki went on. "Did he buy it at the same time he bought the saloon from Dutch John?"

"Yes. I do know that."

"Who's staying in the rooms downstairs, then?"

"Some men he sent here to start the work, I guess."

Ki concluded that the vague answers he'd gotten so far were believable, but he could not decide whether Cheri was as honestly innocent of knowledge about her mysterious employer as she seemed to be, or whether she was playing a deeper game. He decided to risk a little further probing.

"I'm sure you know who's staying in those downstairs rooms, Cheri. Suppose you tell me who they are, and the kind of work they've come here to do."

Cheri's thoughtful frown returned. "I don't know what kind of work Frank's planning on having them do, but I think it's some kind of building job that he hasn't started yet."

"What about the men?"

"Oh, they come into the saloon, but they keep to themselves. I haven't had much to do with them, because they're a pretty rough bunch. Like—" Cheri stopped short, her eyes widening.

Suddenly suspicious, Ki stabbed in the dark. "Like those two who tried to start a fight with us yesterday?"

Cheri's startled expression told Ki all he needed to know. Keeping his own face carefully blank, he asked her, "They're both men your boss has sent here, aren't they?"

"Yes," she admitted reluctantly. "But they were just mean drunk yesterday, Ki! It wouldn't have mattered who was passing by, they'd still have tried to make trouble!"

Ki's questions had confirmed his suspicions. By now he was convinced that the mysterious Frank Jeffers was an agent of the cartel. He was also sure that Cheri did not even suspect the existence of the sinister organization, and knew nothing of her boss's connection with it. He concluded that it was time to follow the lead she'd unwittingly given him, and concentrate on Jeffers.

"I suppose you're right," he said, his voice casual. "But I think I'll keep the job I've got. You can see there'd always be trouble if I tried work on the same job with two men I had that run-in with yesterday."

Cheri nodded, frowning thoughtfully. "Yes. Yes, I can see that, Ki." Her frown deepened and she went on, "I hope you're not just going to disappear now. You aren't, are you?"

"Of course not. But I do have to leave."

"Not right this minute, though," she said. "Even if you're wide awake by now, I promised—"

Ki caught her wrist as Cheri reached for him, and said, "We can let your promise wait until next time, Cheri. I have work to do, and I'd hate to be responsible for your neglecting the saloon and getting into trouble with your boss."

"But you promise there'll be a next time?"

72

"Of course." Ki rolled off the bed and started dressing. He went on, "I'll be back looking for you very soon."

Cheri had lain back on the bed when Ki got up. She fought back a yawn before saying, "You can't come back too soon, Ki. I can't remember knowing a man who's made me feel as good as I do now." This time she yawned without trying to suppress it. "Ki, you won't have any trouble finding your way out, will you? I've just got to have a little nap before I go to work."

"Sleep, then," Ki told her. "I can let myself out all right."

Cheri was asleep before Ki left the room. He crossed the silk-draped chamber, going unerringly to the door. His mind was still on Cheri. He was thinking that he felt almost as relaxed as she did, and he was smiling as he opened the outer door and stepped onto the tiny, dark landing. Had be been as alert as usual, less relaxed, Ki's cat-quick reflexes might have saved him, but the almost inaudible scraping of boot soles on the board floor of the landing came only a split second before the blackjack struck his head. Without a sound, Ki crumpled to the floor.

"We're just wasting our time poking through stuff in this dusty basement," Captain Tinker told Jessie. "This courthouse wasn't even built when I handed out most of those deeds. The county just had a littled shed on the back of the square, then. That jackass, Zeke Carter, might be telling the truth when he says he doesn't know anything about them."

"Then why are some pages missing from those bound recordbooks the law requires him to keep?" Jessie asked.

"People aren't always careful, Jessie. Clerks before this one might've spoiled some entries, spilled ink on the pages, or something like that."

"Just the same, we've got to keep looking," Jessie said.

"I guess we do, at that."

Tinker leaned his cane against the box of papers they'd just finished sorting through. Limping the few steps nec-

73

essary, he went to the corner and started dragging another of the heavy wooden crates toward the area they'd cleared to work in.

Jessie hurried to help him. They wrestled the box into the circle of light cast by the lamp on the high wooden file case, and opened its hinged lid. Folders jammed to bursting with sheets of paper filled the case. The old captain sighed and began lifting them out and handing them to Jessie. She skimmed rapidly through the papers, finished the file, put it aside, and picked up the next one.

"I'm sorry I can't help you more, Jessie," Captain Tinker apologized. "Even when I put on my spectacles, I can't see the way I used to."

"I don't mind that, but this job would be easier if whoever packed these files away had just kept the different kinds of records separate," Jessie remarked. "They're all mixed up—deeds, court cases, expense vouchers for the different offices, payroll lists, sheriff's warrants, tax rolls. It's going to take a long time to go through all of them."

"It's been a long day," Tinker agreed. "Suppose we just stop right now and start again tomorrow?" He hauled a thick, silver-cased watch from his pocket and flipped its cover open. "Five o'clock. By the time we get home, Martha's going to have supper on the table."

"That's the best idea I've heard since noon," Jessie said. "I'm sure all these boxes will still be here tomorrow."

"And I guess we will too," the Captain said, blowing out the lamp.

"Unless Ki uncovers something that will send us in another direction," Jessie replied, standing aside to let the old man start up the stairs ahead of her.

When Jessie and the Captain reached his house, Bobby and his mother were waiting on the porch. Sitting with them was a young man wearing jeans and a denim jacket.

"You haven't had time to meet all my kin," the Captain said to Jessie as he reined in. "The young fellow's my nephew, Martha's brother's boy. Jed Clemson's his name.

74

He works down south on the Abel ranch, when he's not busy on the home place."

Bobby came running out to the buggy. "I'll drive around to the barn and unhitch, Grandpa," he said. "Jed's going to stay for supper. He says he's got something to tell you."

Introductions were made on the veranda, and when the formalities had been completed, Jed Clemson said, "Clegg told me you was here, Miss Starbuck. He's the one talked to you when you stopped yesterday at the south pass. I'd sure like it if you'd tell me about your Circle Star ranch down in Texas. I guess I've heard Uncle Bob mention it a thousand times."

"You won't have to ask me twice to talk about the Circle Star," Jessie smiled. "It's my favorite place."

"Jessie can tell you what it's really like, too," Tinker said. "All I told you was second-hand, things I heard about from her father."

Watching Jed as he listened to the Captain, Jessie put his age at within year or so of her own. He spoke softly, but his voice had a hint of the authority it might one day carry. His features were regular, he was neither handsome nor ugly. He stood tall and was well-muscled, with the capable hands and bronzed complexion of one who works hard outdoors. Jed Clemson was, she thought, the kind of man Bobby would grow into.

When they'd moved indoors to the parlor, the Captain said, "Jed, I hear you've got something on your mind. Bobby told me you did, anyhow."

"Now don't get started on a lot of long-winded talking," Martha broke in before Jed could reply. "Supper's ready to dish up, soon as Ki gets here. You can do your talking later, Captain."

"We don't have to wait for Ki," Jessie said. "He might not be here for another hour. I'm sure the Captain and Bobby and Mr. Clemson are hungry, and to tell the truth, so am I."

"Why don't we go ahead, then, Martha?" the Captain

said. "If Jessie's sure Ki won't feel slighted. And I'm sure Jed will be more comfortable if you don't call him 'mister.'"

"That's right," Jed agreed.

"Fine. And I answer better to Jessie. And Ki won't mind a bit," Jessie assured them. "You can keep something warm for him, Martha, if he doesn't get here in time to join us."

"That won't be a bit of trouble," Martha said. "You and Jessie'll want to wash, and Bobby will too, when he gets back from the barn. I'll have supper on the table by the time you're ready to sit down."

At the table, Jessie and Jed did most of the talking. He was full of questions about the Circle Star and the cross-breeding experiments that Alex Starbuck had begun and Jessie was still carrying on. Bobby broke in now and then with a comment about his brief stay there, and the Captain made an occasional remark, while Martha was silent except for her urgings to everyone to eat another bite of this or that. The meal was completed down to pie and coffee before Jessie realized that Ki still had not shown up.

"I can't understand why Ki's so late," she said. "Of course, he didn't tell me when he planned to be back, but he never does at the ranch, either. I suppose he must have run into some sort of lead he's trying to track down."

"From what I heard about him taking care of those two men at the saloon yesterday, you don't have to worry about him," the Captain said.

"I'm not worried," Jessie replied. "Ki can certainly take care of himself. But he's also very considerate. If he hadn't intended to be back for supper, I'm sure he'd have told Martha."

"Now don't go worrying about me, either, Jessie," Martha said. "I've got Ki's supper in the oven, and it'll stay hot till he gets here. Now, you and the Captain and Jed go on in the parlor, I know you want to talk. Bobby's going to help with the dishes."

As they moved to the parlor, Jessie said to Jed, "If you'd

like to talk privately with Captain Tinker, I'll be glad to sit on the veranda and watch for Ki."

"I'd like for you to stay with us," Jed replied. "Aunt Martha said you'd come here to help Uncle Bob do something about that damned—excuse me—that railroad, so I guess it concerns you about like it does us folks who live here."

When they'd settled into chairs in the tidy parlor, Captain Tinker began filling his pipe and said, "You might as well start unshipping your cargo, Jed. What's got you upset?"

"That fellow Prosser's been out to talk to the folks again," Jed replied. "Dad was in the fields yesterday, and I'd already started for the ranch, so he caught Mother by herself. She was so nervous when Dad got back to the house that it took him nearly an hour to get her calmed down enough to talk about it."

"What in tunket did Prosser say to her?" Tinker asked, scowling.

"I don't know that it was *what* he said as much as how he said it, Uncle Bob," Jed said. "She'd settled down by the time I got home, but I could see she was still on edge."

"Did he threaten your mother, Jed?" Jessie asked.

"Not in so many words, as nearly as I could make out. But he did a lot of hinting about how terrible accidents happen to people on farms. Then he said that the best thing Dad could do at his age was to move into town where he'd be safe."

"Did he offer to buy you folks out?" the Captain asked.

"Not outright, Uncle Bob. To tell you the truth, I'd have run the son of—well, I'd have run him off, if I'd been there, and Dad would've too, if he hadn't been out working."

Jessie said thoughtfully, "If he didn't make an outright threat and link it with an offer to buy you out, I don't think there's much you can do, Jed." The mantel clock struck eight as Jessie was talking, and she looked at it and said,

77

"I can't understand why Ki's so late."

"You know, Jed," Captain Tinker said, "I'd give up that job you've got out at Abel's and stay—" He stopped short as a deep-toned bell started clamoring in the distance. "That's the firebell! Let's go take a look outside!"

For a moment after they'd trooped out to the yard and begun scanning the sky, they saw no sign of a blaze. Then Bobby pointed behind the house with an excited shout, and everyone turned to look at the angry red glow that was rising.

"Oh, my God!" Jed exclaimed. "It looks like it's our house burning down!"

Chapter 8

Captain Tinker responded to Jed's words with the swift reactions he'd acquired during long years of command.

"You must've come here on your horse, Jed," he said. "Go on, don't wait for us. Jessie, go tell Bobby to meet me in the barn and help me harness the buggy. Tell Martha she'd best stay here. Ki might get back while we're gone."

Within ten minutes of the time when they'd first heard the firebell tolling, Captain Tinker was urging his horse to greater speed while Jessie and Bobby tried to keep their seats in the buggy as it bounced, rocked, and jolted over the unpaved road in the direction of the fire.

Other Hidden Valley residents were on the way too. The buggy passed several slower vehicles and a straggle of pedestrians; a number of men on horseback galloped past them. By the time they'd left behind the town's last streets, the northwestern sky was a solid glare of pulsing, menacing red. Jessie could not locate the exact center of the blaze against the sky's almost uniform hue, but with his experienced eyes, Captain Tinker had taken bearings on the location of the fire when it was young, a single blotch of red against the darkness.

"That's not Clemson's house burning," he called to his passengers. "Too far west. Most likely it's the Garvey place." He hauled on the reins and the buggy trembled to a stop. "Bobby, you run back and tell your mother. She'll be worrying herself sick, thinking it might be Harry and Alice's house."

Bobby opened his mouth to protest, but thought better of it and hopped out of the buggy. The captain geed the horse ahead and shoehorned the buggy back into the thickening flow of vehicles that now clogged the narrow dirt road.

Even before they turned off into the lane that led to the burning farmhouse, Jessie and the old man saw the red sky slowly fading to a malignant orange hue and growing darker as the flames consuming the dwelling began to lose intensity.

"Too bad," the Captain said. "House is most likely lost. They go fast, once they start. A few buckets of wellwater don't do much good after a fire's begun to make headway."

Jessie had seen fires in isolated buildings too, and knew the truth of Tinker's words. She nodded silently, keeping her eyes on the steadily waning blaze. The vehicles ahead of them had already begun to slow down, and by the time they reached a point where they could see the burning house, only its framing timbers still burned.

Silhouetted against the flames were the figures of men darting back and forth. Some of them had buckets, and when one of them braved the heat and ran in close to dash water on the dying red tongues, white clouds of steam arose. Beyond the house they could see other men and a few women carrying burlap sacks, and a half-dozen men with sacks had climbed to the roof of the main barn; these were

80

busy beating out the occasional sparks and embers that the light night breeze carried toward them.

"Lucky the wind wasn't blowing hard. They'd have lost the barns and sheds too, if it had been," Captain Tinker said. Then he grunted and added, "That's little enough help, with the house gone, but at least they'll have something to start from."

"Are you sure they'll rebuild?" Jessie asked.

"Sure enough. It's their home place."

"I wasn't thinking of it that way," she replied. "If the railroad company's offered to buy them out, would they take the money and start over somewhere else?"

"Would you, if that was the house on your place burning?"

"No," Jessie said after a moment's thought. "No, I'm sure I wouldn't."

They'd reached the point now where hastily tethered horses, wagons, buggies, and an occasional shay or closed carriage had stopped in a confused crisscross array, and the buggy could go no further. Reining in, the Captain looped the leathers around the whipsocket. He reached for his cane, and Jessie jumped nimbly from the buggy and helped the old man down. She followed him to a huddle of women who stood at one side, watching the burning framework.

As they drew closer, Jessie saw that the group had formed around the few pieces of furniture that had been carried from the house during the first moments after the fire started. The salvage was pitifully meager. There were two or three straight chairs, a Boston rocker, a small table, a marble-topped commode, a child's desk, a hatrack. On the ground beside the furniture, a few odds and ends of dishes and cooking utensils were scattered.

Sitting in the rocking chair, a shawl around her shoulders, a woman was staring dry-eyed at the dying flickers of flame that still shot out thin red tongues from the few wall studs that were now all that remained of the house. Before Jessie and the Captain reached the group, they stopped and turned to look when shouts rose from the men who were still fighting the fire.

The firefighters were running from the blaze, and they saw the reason at once. The rafters were sagging, drooping sadly downward. Within a few seconds after the first warning shout, the flaming rafters cracked with a series of small explosions like sharp pistol shots, and the heavy framing timbers, which were all that remained of the roof, crashed to the ground, dragging with them a few of the wall studs. A tower of fresh flame, studded with big sparks that glowed like bright stars against the dark sky, flared up from the fallen timbers.

A sighing murmur rose from the group huddled around the bits of furniture. It was quickly overriden by the shouts of firefighters, who rushed back with their buckets and bags to douse the triangle of bright flames that had suddenly begun to dance between the studding that remained standing. Jessie and the Captain watched for a moment before moving on to join the group around the salvaged household goods.

Captain Tinker hobbled to the rocker and put his hand on the shoulder of the stonefaced woman sitting in it. He said, "We're all as sorry as can be, Rose. Count on Martha and me to help any way we can."

"Thank you, Captain," she replied. "I guess it could've been worse. Jethro and me are still alive. The barn and the sheds didn't go, and the stock's all saved. We'll make out."

"How'd it start, Rose?" he asked.

"Dear only knows. One minute me and Jethro was in the bedroom getting ready to go to bed, and the next minute there was fire all around the house on the outside."

"It didn't start from a flue, the kitchen, maybe?" he asked. "Or a stove in the parlor?"

Rose Garvey shook her head. "No. I've been wondering while I sat here how it begun."

"And you're sure it wasn't from a flue?"

"Sure as sure, Captain. I let the kitchen fire die out after

82

I'd cooked supper. That was around sundown, and when Jethro heard the clock in the parlor strike nine, he said it was bedtime. And the only stove that's been lit since the weather turned at summer was that one in the kitchen."

"No, it couldn't have been a flue, then," Tinker said, as much to himself as to Rose Garvey and Jessie. He went on, "Fires don't start by themselves, though. There's got to be a reason." He took Jessie's arm and led her a step or two away from the group. "You live outdoors a lot, and you've got to be smart, seeing you're Alex Starbuck's daughter. I want you to do something for me, Jessie."

"Anything you ask, Captain."

"That fire's just about out now. In a few minutes, when the fuss around the house dies down, you go up and walk around a little bit. Take your time, and use your eyes and nose."

"Nose?"

"You've smelled a place on the ground where somebody's used coal oil to start a fire, haven't you, Jessie?"

"I smell that every branding season. We use coal oil at the Circle Star to kindle our branding fires fast. There's so little wood around there that we don't have any kindling."

"Then you know what you'll be trying to find."

"You think the fire was set, don't you, Captain Tinker?"

"If it didn't start in a flue, it had to be."

"Yes, of course," Jessie replied thoughtfully.

"You don't have to say anything about what you've found, if you find anything at all. We'll talk about it later."

Jessie nodded. The Captain did not have to tell her that the Garvey farm spread over land that would be needed by the railroad for their right-of-way through the north pass out of Hidden Valley.

When Captain Tinker went back to rejoin the group around Rose Garvey, Jessie made her way toward the burned skeleton that had once been a house. Other spectators, late arrivals, were beginning to go up to the ruins for a close look, and most of the men who'd been fighting the blaze were standing near the skeleton with their gear at hand to use if a gust of wind should cause a sudden flareup. The men who'd been on the barn were coming down the high ladder that leaned against the building, and in the moving, shifting crowd, no one paid attention to Jessie.

Begining at the corner of the house nearest her, Jessie moved slowly along its end, scanning the ground closely, stopping occasionally to bend down and sniff the parched soil. She'd covered the end and was halfway around the rear, near the spot where the back door had been, before she found what the Captain had suspected. Here, Garvey had built a flagstone walkway to the well. A few feet from the house, the walk split into a Y, and one arm going to the well, the other to the barn. In the angle where the Y began, the unmistakable odor of coal oil was very strong.

Though large stretches of live coals glowed redly on many of the studs that remained erect, and there were coals in the center of the devastated dwelling where the rafters had collapsed, the flames had almost completely died away. Darkness obscured detail on the ground around the walk, and Jessie dropped to her knees, trying to see whether obvious traces of the liquid remained on the ground or the flagstone. Bending down, her head close to the ground, she could see a faint sheen of the oil on one of the flat stones that made up the walk.

A man's voice broke into her concentration, asking, "Did you lose something, Jessie?"

Looking up into the gloom, Jessie recognized Jed Clemson standing a short distance away. She said, "No. Captain Tinker asked me to look for something."

"From the looks of things, you've found it."

"I think I have." She hesitated for a moment, then decided it wasn't likely that the Captain would object to her sharing what she'd found with his nephew. She said, "Come here and look and smell the ground, Jed. See if I'm right."

"Right about what?" Jed asked. He came to where Jessie

was kneeling, and hunkered down beside her. His eyes followed her finger, pointed at the stained flagstone. He bent forward, lowered his head, and sniffed. "Coal oil."

"That's what the Captain asked me to look for."

"He suspects somebody set the house afire?"

"What he said was that if the fire didn't start in a flue, someone must have started it from outside. And Mrs. Garvey told us that the fire in her kitchen stove went out hours ago."

"You and Captain Bob have been busy while I was up on the barn roof," Jed commented. He looked at the smeared stone in thoughtful silence. "Captain Bob's generally right," he said. He extended his hand to help Jessie rise. "Come on, let's go tell him about this."

"Let's do it quietly, though, Jed, where nobody else can hear us," Jessie suggested. She took Jed's hand and pulled herself to her feet. "I'm not sure the Captain wants anybody else to know just yet that the fire was deliberately set."

They rounded the corner of the house. A half-dozen lanterns had been lighted by now, but compared to the brilliance that the burning house had so recently shed on the scene, the lanterns were as ineffective as fireflies in dispelling the gloom. There were very few men still keeping watch on the dying embers now; all but two or three had joined the crowd clustered around the chair where Rose Garvey sat.

Jessie and Jed began working their way through the crowd. As they drew closer to its center, Jessie saw that a man with a soot-smeared face stood beside Captain Tinker, behind the chair in which Mrs. Garvey was sitting. Jessie could see that the man who was standing facing them had obviously not been among those fighting the fire. His coat looked bandbox-fresh, and a clean white collar gleamed below the brim of the gray derby that he'd pushed to the back of his head. The faces of the Captain and the Garveys were turned toward the newcomer, and as Jessie and Jed

85

drew closer, she could hear what the man was saying. She knew who he was then, and didn't need Jed's whispered indentification.

"That's Prosser, the land agent for the railroad," he said.

"I had an idea that was who he was," she replied. "Come on, Jed. Let's get up to where we can whisper to the Captain and tell him what we found." They began wiggling through the crowd.

Prosser was saying persuasively, "Now you don't want to rebuild here, I'm sure. Why, this place will always have unhappy memories for you, Mrs. Garvey. If you take my offer, you can buy a farm somewhere else and build a fine new house, buy brand-new furniture, everything you need to give you a fresh start. You won't always be reminded of what happened to you here."

"I'd as soon stay," Rose Garvey said quietly. "And I imagine Jethro would too."

"Certain sure, I would!" Garvey said emphatically.

"It's a lot of money I'm offering you," Prosser told him.

"They don't want your money, Prosser," Captain Tinker said. "But I guess a man like you wouldn't understand how most folks feel about a place they've built with their own hands and lived in for twenty or so years."

"Tinker, you stay out of this!" Prosser snapped.

"I'm in it up to my scuppers already, and I intend to stay in it!" the Captain shot back. "There's miles and miles of land around this Valley where you can put your railroad tracks down. Go someplace else, and leave these folks alone!"

"I'm not talking to you," Prosser retorted. "If you'd stayed out of this from the beginning, Hidden Valley would be a lot better off!" He turned back to the Garveys. "Now I've made you folks a good offer. I know that right now you're both tired and upset, and I'm not going to press you to make up your minds tonight. I'll stop back tomorrow—"

"We won't be here," Garvey said. "We've had offers

86

from a lot of folks to stay with them tonight, and we'll take one of them as soon as we get a few minutes' peace."

Jessie and Jed had worked their way to Captain Tinker's side while Prosser was talking to the Garveys. The old man looked at Jessie, and his thick white eyebrows went up questioningly. She nodded and moved still closer to his side. Tinker bent toward her.

"You were right, Captain," Jessie whispered in his ear. "It was arson. Jed and I found traces of coal oil behind the house, just outside the back door."

"I was pretty sure there'd be some signs, if we looked close enough," he said. "But it won't do much good unless we can tie it to Prosser, or somebody else connected with the railroad."

"Aren't you going to face Prosser with it?" she asked.

Tinker shook his head. "Not right now. We need a lot more to go on than we've got. You and Jed just keep quiet."

Jessie nodded and returned her attention to the discussion between Prosser and the Garveys.

"I'm trying to do you people a favor," Prosser said. "I'm ready to pay you hard cash, Mr. Garvey, right this minute!" He began taking bundles of banknotes from his coat pockets. Putting them in a thick stack, he waved them in Garvey's face. "Here. This is yours right now, if you take my offer!"

Garvey looked at the stack of money, and then down at his wife. She shook her head. He said, "You got your answer, Mr. Prosser. Now just go away and let us be, will you?"

"You don't seem to understand," Prosser insisted. "I'm offering you a good price for a few acres of farmland and a burned-down shell of a house!"

"You're trying to get hold of our land so your pick-and-shovel crews can rip it up and put down railroad tracks!" Garvey broke in. "You're not pulling any wool over our eyes."

Prosser shook his head sadly. "You folks have just been

listening to a lot of ugly lies." He paused for a moment, then went on, "I'll tell you what I'll do, Mr. Garvey." Groping in his coat pocket, he produced two more sheaves of bills. "I'll raise my last offer by two thousand dollars. That's more than this place of yours was worth with your house still standing."

Garvey bent over his wife's shoulder and asked her, "Does that sound any better to you, Rose?"

She shook her head. "I feel just the same as I did when we were talking before Mr. Prosser got here, Jethro. We'll go ahead and move our stuff into the barn and live there while we're building a new house."

Straightening up, Garvey faced the railroad agent again. "I guess you heard what she said, Mr. Prosser. We won't be taking your offer."

"All right!" Prosser snapped. "But I warn you right now, you'll live to regret this!"

Cramming his derby down on his head, Prosser pushed rudely through the crowd, and while all eyes turned to watch his departure, he found his buggy and drove away.

"Well, he won't bother you anymore for a while," Captain Tinker observed. "And don't worry too much. Things will work out all right."

"We know they will, Captain," Garvey said. "We've had all the furniture we'll need offered to us already, so we can move into the barn right away and be real comfortable."

"And whatever else you need, let me know," Tinker told him. "I'll see that you get it."

"That goes for us too," a fresh voice said behind Jessie.

She and the Captain turned. Jed Clemson and an older couple had moved through the dispersing crowd.

"Jessie, I'd like you to meet my folks," Jed said. "My mother and father. I've been telling them about you."

"I'm Henry Clemson, and this is Alice," Jed's father said. "Both of us feel like we know the Starbuck family as well as we do our own kin, after hearing Bob talk about your father for all these years."

"You'll have to come for supper, when you've got time," Alice Clemson said. "You tell Jed when, and I'll fix you up a real Hidden Valley meal. We don't live too far from here, right over that way."

As she spoke, Mrs. Clemson half-turned and extended her hand to point in the direction of their home. Jessie's eyes followed the pointing finger, and her gasp caused the other to look as well. A patch of red was beginning to color the sky where Alice Clemson was pointing.

Chapter 9

"Oh, dear God, don't let it be our house!" Mrs. Clemson exclaimed. "We left Peony there by herself!"

"It is our house, Alice," Clemson said. His voice was calm, but strained. "Or one of our barns. There's nothing else where that blaze is that would burn. But Peony's able to take care of herself." He turned to Jed. "Bob will look after your mother, Jed. Let's go!"

Jed and Henry Clemson had come on saddle horses to the fire, leaving Mrs. Clemson to follow in a buggy. The departure of the Clemson men, and their shouts as they spurred past the departing firefighters, got help moving fast. Others, of course, had seen the slowly growing patch of red, and were whipping up their horses even before they heard the shouting. What had begun as a leisurely departure became a small stampede as the weary men who'd fought the Garvey fire rushed to quell the new blaze.

This time a series of circumstances combined to make

the firefighters' job easier. They had their transportation ready; no time had to be spent in hitching up a buggy or wagon. Their horses were fresh after having rested for nearly two hours after galloping from town to the first fire, and the distance to the blaze was not quite two miles, instead of more than six.

Most importantly, the Clemson house was built of logs, not boards. The flames could not eat through the solid wood and ignite the walls inside the house, and the lessened intensity of the heat allowed the firefighters to get close, instead of forcing them to attack the flames from a distance. The house's major point of vulnerability was its roof, and the fire had not climbed to the eaves when most of the volunteers arrived.

Jed and Henry had gotten home several minutes ahead of the others leaving the Garvey house. When they'd arrived, they found fifteen-year-old Peony already attacking the blaze, scooping up shovelfuls of dirt from the dry soil a few feet from the house, and tossing the dirt on the wall. Some of the dirt fell to the ground before reaching the wall, but the remainder landed on the house and smothered an area as big as the span of a man's outspread hands. Jed and Henry had wasted no time in running to the barn for shovels and following Peony's example.

When the other men arrived and saw how effective the dirt was in smothering the creeping flames, they adopted the same method. Most of them carried a spade or shovel in their wagons, and many who had buckets used them to scoop up dirt. A solid line of men was soon working shoulder to shoulder along each side. Within less than a half-hour from the time the fire had started, it was being attacked by exhausted but still willing workers.

Where thin, creeping tongues of flame had reached the low eaves and kindled the vulnerable shakes that covered the roof, the men with buckets formed a line from the well to the house and doused the roof. Then the bucket brigade turned its attention to the walls. Thin tongues of smoke were trickling from the logs here and there, where some dormant sparks remained, but these vanished when a bucket of water was splashed on them. Though the flames had girdled almost the entire house when the volunteers arrived from the earlier blaze, the fire was extinguished with surprising speed.

Alice Clemson had been worried and anxious when Captain Tinker's buggy wheeled up and stopped in front of the house, but when she'd seen how quickly the fire was yielding, she said to Jessie, "That fire's not really going to hurt our house, is it?"

"No," Jessie replied. "The log walls are going to save it."

"Then as soon as we're sure it's safe, I'm going to go in and make coffee and see what I've got in the pantry that I can feed those poor men. They haven't had any rest for hours!"

"I think it's perfectly safe to go in now," Jessie said. "You can see the fire's going to be completely out in just a few more minutes. I'll come along and help you."

Between them, Alice and Jessie made coffee and, while it was brewing, sliced what had been left of a beef roast that had been the Clemsons' supper, and made sandwiches. When the firefighters found their job brought to such a quick and unexpected end, they stood around drinking coffee and eating and swapping stories of their experiences in fighting the two fires.

"Let's don't forget to give Peony credit for saving the house, though," Henry Clemson reminded them. "She was so quick to figure out that dirt would put the fire out faster than water, that all the rest of us had to do was follow her example."

"How'd you happen to think of shoveling dirt instead of using water, Peony?" Captain Tinker asked the girl.

"I just remembered when we had picnics and how Papa and Jed put out fire with dirt," Peony replied. "I knew I wasn't strong enough to haul a lot of water up from the well."

92

"You sure did the right thing, sis," Jed said. "But how'd you know the house was on fire? Did you look out the window?"

"No. Well, I did, but I might not have if I hadn't heard somebody outside and looked to see if you and Mama and Papa were coming home." She frowned and added, "I don't remember exactly what I heard, because that was when I saw the fire and got excited."

"You didn't see anybody running away?" her father asked.

"No, sir." Peony frowned. "There wasn't any fire when I first went to the window, either. It seemed like it started all at once, right about the time I looked out."

"Well, if we had any doubt about the fire being deliberately set, that oughta settle it," Henry said soberly.

Captain Tinker nodded. "It was set, all right." He turned to Jessie and went on, "Pick up that lantern, Jessie, and let's walk around and take a close look at those walls."

Any doubts they might have had vanished when the group fell in behind the Captain and Jessie and started walking around the house, inspecting the scars left by the fire. The pattern of the flames was marked clearly by the charred areas.

"Somebody walked along there with a bucket of coal oil and splashed it on the wall," Captain Tinker said, pointing with his cane at the series of burned arcs that ran along the wall. "You men have seen what happens when you slosh a bucket of water on a wall. It makes a mark just like this, a curve where most of the water hits, and a wider streak where it spreads when it runs down. Only this wasn't water running down, it was coal oil."

Jessie had been holding the lantern close to the logs at the top of one of the arcs. Now she said, "You can see something else, if you look closely. A normal fire burns hottest at the bottom, but these burned places are deeper at the top, where there was the most coal oil on the logs."

"And there's not any question about it," Jed said. He put his hand on his sister's shoulder. "Peony saved our house."

93

"No doubt about that," Tinker agreed. He turned to the others and went on, "I haven't had time until now to tell you men that whoever set the Garvey place on fire started that one with coal oil too. Jessie found proof of that, places where there were coal-oil smears on the flagstones of that path Jethro built back of his house."

"It's that damned railroad outfit," one of the volunteers said grimly. "What we oughta do is catch that son of a bitch Prosser and douse *him* with coal oil and touch a match to him."

"That wouldn't do a bit of good." Captain Tinker exchanged glances with Jessie, who still stood beside him, holding the lantern. Jessie understood the question in his look, and nodded. The Captain went on, "If we got rid of Prosser, the railroad would just send somebody else to take his place."

"That might be," growled the man who'd just spoken. "But Colt and Winchester can turn out cartridges quicker than the railroad can find rowdies and hire 'em."

"The Captain's right," Jed Clemson said. "The railroad wants the land around the passes, and if Prosser can't buy it, they're ready to take it."

"It'll be a cold day in hell before I sell 'em any land of mine," one of the others growled. "Prosser's been nosing around my place too, trying to buy me out, but I say let 'em put their damned tracks someplace else."

"They quit offering to buy my place," a third put in. "Now they're threatening to go to law and take it away from me because they claim I ain't got a deed to the land."

"Can they do that, Captain Tinker?" asked the man who'd started the discussion.

"Maybe so and maybe not," Tinker replied. "But every one of you men bought your land from me, and if you'll remember, I told you to be sure to take the deeds I gave you and file them at the courthouse. If you did that, the railroad couldn't touch you."

"Deed or no deed," the man grumbled, "it's a damned

94

poor law that don't let a man keep what he's bought and paid for."

"A man named Dickens wrote a book once where he said the law is a jackass, Ben," Tinker said with a wry grin. "I suppose he was right about it, not that it helps us any right this minute."

"What we'd better do up here is what the ranchers are doing at the south pass," Jed said. "They've got men standing guard day and night to keep the railroad from setting foot on any land they haven't bought and paid for."

"Now I'd go right along with that," agreed the man who'd mentioned Colt and Winchester. He turned to Captain Tinker. "If you want to give us a hand, Cap'n, you'd get a bunch of us set up in a posse that could do like the ranchers are."

"It might come down to that in the end," Tinker admitted. "But before we go that far, wouldn't it be smarter if we used the law to help us instead of trying to set up our own law?"

"Just how do you mean that?"

"You men haven't had a chance yet to meet this little lady here," Tinker said, indicating Jessie. "Most of you know where I got the land I sold you, there's not many who haven't heard me talk about Alex Starbuck. This is Miss Jessie Starbuck, and she's come to Nevada Territory all the way from Texas to help me prove that by law I had a right to sell your land to you."

"How's that going to help if the law's on the side of the railroad?" asked the advocate of Colt and Winchester.

Jessie said quietly, "I'm sure that right now I've got all the legal evidence Captain Tinker needs to prove you're the real owners of the land you bought from him."

"That's all well and good, Miss Starbuck, but how's it going to keep the railroad's nightriders from doing what they did over to the Garvey place and tried to do right here to the Clemsons?"

"Without the law behind us, we're like the railroad's nightriders," Jessie replied. "When the law's on our side,

95

we can get help from everybody from the sheriff and the governor on up to the President of the United States."

One of the men guffawed and said sarcastically, "You don't expect us to believe you'd march up to the President and tell him a bunch of poor dirt farmers like us, way out here in Nevada Territory, was looking for him to give us a hand!"

"No," Jessie replied coolly. "Although I've met President Hayes and have had the honor of dining with him and Mrs. Hayes in the White House, I don't believe we'll have to go that high for help. But if I have to, I certainly will!"

Suppressing a chuckle, Captain Tinker said, "Jessie means what she says, too! I'd advise you men to listen to her."

For a moment there was silence while the men who were clustered around Jessie and the Captain exchanged glances. Then one of them said, "I guess we're of a mind to listen, Miss Starbuck, if you've got anything you want to tell us."

"Well, I'm not going to tell you what you'd like to hear, that this fight with the railroad is going to be won tomorrow," she said soberly. "But I'll guarantee that we can win it, if you're willing to have just a little patience."

"It's hard to be patient when they're setting fire to our houses, Jessie," Henry Clemson said. "But I know you're right, and I'm willing to wait awhile, if you're so certain we'll win."

"I'm sure. And as for the fires and the nightriders, I'm sure all you men have guns, and I'd advise you sleep lightly and be ready to shoot if you get any unwanted visitors at night. Nobody's going to blame you for protecting your homes."

"Well, that makes sense," one of the group said. "But what about Prosser?"

"Leave Prosser to the Captain and me," Jessie replied. "We started working today on a job that will help you stop him. Just give us a little time to finish what we've started. But right now it's late and we're all tired, and I think the

96

best thing we can do is get some sleep and save talking for later."

"That's the smartest thing I've heard all night," the Captain seconded. "If you men are of a mind to, we can have a meeting real soon and iron everything out."

"You tell us when it's time to meet, Captain," Clemson said. "I'd imagine we'll all be on hand."

Tinker thought for a moment, then said, "Jessie and I have got some business we need to finish at the courthouse tomorrow—that's really today, I guess. We could all stand a little bit of rest, so how about tomorrow night?"

"It's already tomorrow," Jessie smiled. "Don't you mean tonight, Captain?"

"I guess I do, at that," Tinker replied. He looked at the others and asked, "Is that too soon? Remember, we don't have any days to waste right now."

"That sounds to me like a good time," Jed said. "It'll give me a chance to ride down to the south valley and invite Blaine Abel and some of the other ranchers to come up."

"Anybody got any objections?" the captain asked. He waited a moment, and when no one spoke, he said, "All right. My barn's not as big as some of yours, but it's right in town. That suit all of you men?" When there was a scattering of yesses and no one objected, he nodded. "It's settled, then. About seven."

A few at a time, the exhausted firefighters straggled to their vehicles and horses and started home. Captain Tinker sighed as he watched the last of the vehicles roll away.

"I'd say we put out more than two fires," he told Jessie and the Clemsons. "Those men were at a point where one little move by Prosser or anybody else connected with the railroad would have started a flare-up."

"I think you've started another fire too," Jessie suggested. "One that's going to spread over the entire valley. But it's the kind of fire we need to stop the—" She'd been about to say *cartel,* but caught herself in time to substitute

97

a word the Clemsons would be quicker to understand. "—to stop the railroad from doing a great deal of damage to a lot of people."

It was not until she and the Captain had said their good-byes to the Clemson family and turned onto the road to town that Jessie realized that since they'd left for the first fire she'd been too busy to think about Ki.

"I certainly hope we'll find Ki at your house when we get there," she said. "It may have been a mistake for him to go back to that saloon. After the run-in we had with those two hardcases there yesterday, he might walk into more trouble."

"Things don't really get lively in most saloons until after supper, Jessie. Don't worry so much. I imagine Ki's all right."

At that particular moment, Ki was anything but all right. He had regained consciousness and opened his eyes to find himself in total darkness. There was no way for him to know how long he had been unconscious, Ki realized. The afternoon had been very late when he'd left Cheri, and the darkness could indicate that it was now night, or that he was confined in a cellar.

All that Ki was sure of was that he was lying on his back on a hard surface. He moved, and for an instant his head felt as though a bolt of lightning had struck it. He forced himself to relax, and after a few moments the pain settled down to a painful throbbing. Instinctively he started to bring a hand up to his head, and discovered that his wrists were tied together tightly and that his hands had no feeling.

Closing his eyes, he waited for the throbbing to subside, and moved again. This time the stabbing surges in his head were less intense. After he'd moved his arms experimentally and found the pain bearable, Ki started to roll onto his side. When he moved his legs to get the necessary leverage, he learned that his ankles were also lashed together.

Moving clumsily because of his bonds, Ki finally succeeded in rolling. He felt the floor, but his numb fingers could not identify its composition. It could have been brick, wood, cement, or even paper. Levering himself into a sitting position, he looked around. He thought, but could not be absolutely sure, that in two small areas high above his head he could detect a difference in the density of the blackness that surrounded him. All he could really be sure of, Ki thought ruefully, was that wherever he was confined, its darkness was total.

Having reached that conclusion, Ki closed his eyes again. Having closed them, he thought with wry amusement that habit was strong. Then he began thinking seriously about the logical succession of moves to be made. There were so few that his meditation was brief. There were only two moves indicated for the moment: get rid of his bonds and discover where he was.

Flexing his forearm muscles and twisting his wrists with all the strength he could muster produced a tiny, almost infinitesimal amount of slack. Small as it was, the slack restored part of Ki's circulation, and when he tried to open and close his hands, he could now feel them move. After he'd flexed his fingers for a few moments, the numbness that had deprived him of a sense of touch began to diminish. Ki put his fingertips on the floor, and after rubbing them on its surface for several minutes, he could identify it as being made from bare boards.

Ki's training in unarmed combat had taught him how flexible the human body can be; by exercising the control he'd acquired through years of exacting discipline, even with his wrists bound he could reach almost as far and move his arms almost as freely as he could when they were not tied.

He felt his vest pockets and discovered that whoever had slugged and tied him had not searched him well, apparently only patting him down; they had not discovered the *shuriken* he'd concealed in some of the many pockets of his vest. They were flat and made no bulge at all, so a casual search might not reveal them, and in any case they might not be recognized as weapons. He had no difficulty in taking one of the throwing blades from a pocket. Using its razor-sharp edges, he severed the bonds around his wrists. After that, freeing his ankles was easy.

Ki made his mind blank for the next few minutes, which he spent going through the basic mind-control exercises he'd begun learning as a child. He limbered up his body then, beginning with the simplest body movements and advancing by stages to the moves requiring full coordination of his hands, feet, limbs, head, and torso. When he was finally satisfied, his circulation was again normal, and the usual suppleness had returned to his joints, and fully-controlled strength to his muscles.

Now, Ki thought to himself in the darkness, *Now that I am ready, I must discover where I am, and then move myself to where I wish to be.*

★

Chapter 10

Although she was tired after her exertions at the two fires
and did not get to bed until the early hours of the morning,
Jessie slept badly. When she and the Captain reached his
house and found that Ki still had neither returned nor sent
a message, Jessie had wanted to start looking for him at
once. Finally she agreed with Captain Tinker that searching
for Ki during the predawn hours would be futile, and went
to bed. Her sleep was restless, and she awoke fully when
dawn began to brighten the sky. She tossed and turned,
trying to go back to sleep, but could not.

Throwing aside the sheet that covered her, Jessie slipped
out of the bed and stood beside it for a moment, stretching
her arms above her head, rising on her toes. She blinked
her green eyes to dispel the last traces of drowsiness and
threw back her head, letting her mane of tawny gold hair
fall free down her back.

From chin to shoulders to breasts and torso and thighs,

her flawless skin radiated vitality. The svelte contours of her limbs gave no hint of the strong muscles they concealed. Jessie's full breasts stood firm and proud, their pink nipples stiffening in the cool morning air. The sweep of her flat abdomen into the flare of her hips and the taper of hips into thighs showed woman's form in man's ideal of beauty.

Only Jessie's wide green eyes, the blush of health on her cheeks, the glowing rosy tips of her breasts, and the glint of gold from her hair reflected in the tawny curls at her groin showed that she was a living woman. In the filtered light of the bedroom, her naked body had the classic lines of a statue carved in Carrara marble by a master sculptor.

Jessie dressed quickly. She slid her legs into short pantalettes, stepped into the skirt of her green tweed suit, and thrust her feet into trim brown cordovan boots. After buttoning on a fresh off-white silk blouse, she opened the door quietly and stepped into the hall. The door of Ki's bedroom, at the end of the corridor, was ajar. Jessie did not bother to look in the room; if Ki had come in, the door would have been closed. In any case he would have awakened her at once in spite of the hour, to tell her what he'd found out.

Going back into her own room, Jessie slid her double-barreled derringer from beneath her pillow and tucked it into the top of one of her boots. She opened her travel bag and took out the gunbelt and holstered revolver that had been her father's gift. She did not swing out the cylinder to check the loads in the .38 Colt on its .44 frame. Experience had taught Jessie that an unloaded gun was as useful as a caveman's wooden club.

After buckling on her gunbelt, Jessie donned her suit jacket and picked up her wide-brimmed Stetson, but did not put it on. As an afterthought, she took a box of ammunition from her bag and dropped a handful of cartridges into her jacket pocket. She went quietly down the hall to the kitchen door, and when she opened it, she was surprised to see Martha Tinker sitting at the table with a coffee cup in front of her.

"You woke early, too," Jessie said.

"I always do." Martha's smile did not completely hide her worried frown. She stepped to the stove and filled a cup for Jessie from the graniteware coffeepot. "But I'm up a mite earlier than usual today. I didn't sleep so good."

"Neither did I," Jessie confessed.

"Ki?"

Jessie nodded. "If he'd been free to do what he wanted to, he would have sent me a message of some kind, Martha. And he was planning to go back to the saloon yesterday afternoon."

"That's what the Captain said last night when you got back," Martha said. Without asking or being asked, she had sliced bacon from a slab that lay on a shelf beside the kitchen range and put it in a skillet on the stove. The bacon was already beginning to sizzle, and as she broke an egg into the pan, Martha went on, "That saloon's a good place to stay away from. It's a scandal to the town the way it's changed since Dutch John sold it. Rowdies and roughs and worse, I guess, have just taken it over."

"Yes." Jessie sipped the fragrant coffee. "Ki and Bobby and I met some of them on our way into town, remember."

"If that's where you intend to go now, I'd better rouse the Captain. Even at this time of day, that's no place for you to go alone."

Jessie shook her head. "No, Martha. He needs to rest. He had a very long day and a hard night, and he's not a young man anymore. Even if he should wake up and want to come looking for me, don't let him."

"But, Jessie—"

"No," Jessie repeated firmly. "And please don't suggest that I take Bobby along, Martha." She pulled her jacket aside to show the holstered Colt. "I'm well prepared to handle any kind of trouble I might run into."

Martha sighed. "Well, I suppose you know best, Jessie. But I'll worry about you until you come back."

"I'll come back in good shape," Jessie promised. Then,

103

her jaw set firmly and her green eyes crackling with fire, she added, "And when I do come back, Ki will be with me!"

Reminding himself of the adage that even a journey of ten thousand miles begins with a single step, Ki began exploring the midnight-dark room in which he'd found himself confined.

He started at a corner and felt his way along the wall, moving in carefully spaced paces and counting his steps. His fingers told him two things as he edged slowly along, feeling for clues by sliding his hand against the surface. The room was large, and it was not a basement or a cellar. He could feel the cracks between horizontal boards, and the dents made in the wood where nails had been hammered to hold the boards to wall studs. The wood surface had a neutral temperature, neither warm nor cold, which ruled out a basement room, for wooden basement walls were always chilly to the touch.

Until he got midway along the second wall, Ki wondered why such a large room would be without windows or doors. Then he reached one of the two spots he'd noted when he first revived, where the quality of the darkness was different from the dense blackness elsewhere. At close range he could see a lessening of the darkness. The patch was not bright, or even gray, but was infinitesimally less dark than the area around it.

Ki's fingers revealed that the area was defined by a piece of board nailed to the wall. He measured the board by spreading his thumb and middle finger to form a span; the plank was one span wide by four spans long. Ki could think of only one reason why a board should be placed there; the area it covered was too small for a window, so the board must have been nailed over a ventilation opening such as would be found in an attic. The suggestion of light around the edges indicated that night had fallen while Ki was unconscious. In daylight, the tiny crevices between the cover and the inner wall would be brightly outlined. Tugging at the protruding edges of the board, Ki found it unyielding.

Deferring further investigation of the spot until later, Ki completed his circuit of the room. He felt around the second area of lesser darkness; it corresponded exactly with the first in its size and placement. After he'd covered four walls, Ki paused and stood quietly while he mentally summed up his discoveries.

As he'd guessed, the room was large and exactly square, thirty paces on each side. Its size, combined with the covered spots and the absence of a door, led him to an immediate conclusion: he was in the attic of the rooming house to which he'd gone with Cheri. There was no other answer possible.

In an attic, there must be a trapdoor, Ki told himself.

He set about finding it. Stepping out of his slippers, and using the hazy areas of the facing walls to orient himself, he crossed the room diagonally, feeling for a crack or the protruding edge of board that would indicate a trapdoor. He slid his bare feet silently over the floorboards, for he was not sure what lay below the portion of the room where he was confined. There might well be cartel hoodlums in a room below, and any noise he made would bring them running.

His diagonal crossing was unrewarding. Extending an arm at shoulder level, sliding his fingertips along the wall to be sure he did not walk in a curve in the darkness, Ki next walked very slowly, with carefully silent steps, around the room's perimeter. He had covered two sides and was moving along the third when his feet encountered the irregularity he'd been hunting, the edges of the trapdoor that led to the floor below.

Hunkering down, Ki ran his fingers around the square frame. There was no latch, and the top of the door had been finished with boards that leveled it with the floor. The door had no handle, but when Ki made a more painstaking exploration of its surface, he discovered a finger-hole centered

105

near one edge. Inserting a finger, he tugged, but the door was immovable, locked or latched from below.

Sitting down, Ki took a *shuriken* from his jacket pocket and began scraping with one of its star-points from the finger-hole to the near edge of the door. When he'd gouged a groove deep enough to be felt easily in the dark, he scraped from the opposite rim of the fingerhole to the far edge. Ki neither hurried nor wasted any motion. He knew the job would take time, but the trapdoor was his only hope of escaping.

A few shreds and splinters at a time, the hard yellow pine yielded to Ki's patient shaving. He stopped when his labor had scored the cover of the trapdoor to a depth he estimated at just less than a quarter of an inch. Laying the *shuriken* aside, he knelt and inserted the middle finger of his right hand in the hole and grasped his right wrist with his left hand.

Flexing the muscles of his hands and arms with all the strength he could summon, Ki pulled upward. He listened hopefully, willing the wood to crack along the scored vee he'd made, but the door neither creaked nor opened. Standing up, he braced his feet wide apart and tried again, and this time he lifted with his back and shoulder muscles as well as those of his arms, but the result was as disappointing as his first tries had been.

Sitting down, Ki went back to his scraping. The tough wood seemed to grow tougher as the grooves deepened and a greater area came in contact with the tip of the *shuriken*. Patiently, Ki persisted. Measuring by feel, he stopped when his fingertips told him that the groove had deepened to almost a half-inch. He put the *shuriken* aside and stood up to try again.

This time the wood creaked when he applied the first real pressure with his arm muscles, and when he stood up and added the power of his shoulders and back, the wood cracked. A few more hard tugs, and the board split. Ki worked the split open until he could pull the halfboard free from the trapdoor's frame, and used it as a lever to pry up the remaining boards.

Engrossed in his task, Ki had given no thought to the time. He became aware of its passing when he looked down at the trapdoor and saw that it was outlined in gray. He glanced at the boards that covered the openings made to ventilate the attic, and they too were framed in a nimbus of dawn-gray from light that seeped through the crevices between the boards and frame.

Spurred by his success, Ki picked up one of the boards he'd pried from the trapdoor and raised it to use as a hammer in removing the bottom boards. Then a sudden thought held his arm in midair. Hammering would attract the attention of anyone who might be in the big, rambling house. Ki lowered the board and studied this new problem.

A solution popped quickly into Ki's mind. Slipping his vest off, he wrapped it around the board in his hand. He placed one end of the board on the center plank of the trapdoor's bottom, and while he held the board upright with his left hand, he concentrated his vital energy and, forming his hand into a fist, brought it down like a hammer on the top end of the board.

With the end of the vertical board muffled by the horsehide vests, the noise of the impact was no louder than a light cough, but the force of the blow had sprung the plank on which it rested a fraction of an inch. Repositioning the vertical board, Ki struck again. This time the crack opened wide enough for him to get the edge of his improvised lever between the loosened board and the frame and pry it free. The plank popped loose at the end on which Ki had hammered, and hung dangling from the bent nails in its opposite end.

Dropping to the floor, Ki passed his hand through the opening and groped for the latch. He found it after a moment, a heavy bolt, and pulled the barrel back. The trapdoor dropped open, letting a shaft of gray morning light flood the attic.

Ki wasted no time in examining his prison. A ladder had been built on the wall at one side of the trapdoor. Ki pulled on his vest and climbed down.

He found himself on a narrow landing. A door was set in the wall near the foot of the ladder. Ki hesitated, listening with his ear pressed to the door panel. He heard a low murmur, too faint to be recognizable. After straining his ears vainly for several moments and hearing no change in the volume of the noise, Ki tried the doorknob. The door was not locked. Ki pushed carefully. The door swung open silently on well-oiled hinges.

For a moment, Ki listened without moving. The murmur he'd heard earlier had stopped. Stepping through the door, Ki found himself on the landing where he and Cheri had stopped earlier in the day while she unlocked the door that stood a few feet away at the head of a flight of stairs. Ki closed the door that led to the ladder, and saw why he had not noticed it. The door had no knob on the landing side, only a keyhole, and it was set flush, without jambs, which made it appear to be part of the wall.

Stepping across the small landing, Ki pressed his ear to the door that opened into the luxurious, silk-draped chamber with its adjoining bedroom. Now he could hear clearly the voices that had been only a confused murmur. A man was talking. There was something familiar about the voice, but Ki could not identify it from the few words he heard.

". . . before it gets too late," the man said.

"We damn sure can't leave her where she is now," a second man replied. His voice was not as clear as the first man's; it sounded farther away, muffled.

"Why not? All we got to do is lock the door and walk away," the first man said.

"Don't talk like a damn fool, Jug!"

When he heard the name, Ki knew the identities of the men behind the door. Jug was the hulking hoodlum who'd started the fracas in front of the saloon. The other man was almost certainly the one called Slip, whose elbow Ki had dislocated.

"Who's going to come up here?" Jug asked.

"Who do you think? The boss, if he blows into town."

"You know he ain't likely to, Slip," Jug replied. "He said he was going to leave that fellow that's already here to run this job by hisself."

"When he hears how you fucked things up, he's more'n likely to cut a shuck down as fast as he can!" Slip retorted.

"Don't go putting the blame on me, Slip! You was the one that was holding the knife."

"And you shoved her into it!"

"Well, the dirty bitch bit me! Damm it, you could've just held her for me, like I told you to!"

"How in hell did you think I was going to handle her, with one arm all busted up? If you'd been satisfied just to screw her the regular way, like I did—"

"Now, Slip, we been runnin' together long enough for you to know what I like to do to a woman!" Jug protested. "We'd of had to get rid of her anyhow, after we finished."

"But not here, you damn fool! Out in the country someplace, like we always do. We'll take her and the chink in one trip."

"That's a prime idea, Slip! It'll look like he killed her and she killed him. Come on, let's go while it's still dark."

"We been up here ever since we found out about the chink, Jug. That's a long time. Might be it's daylight by now."

"Well, you started to go see if the coast's clear, before we got into this goddamned wrangle! Go look now, while I get this damn blood off my legs!"

Ki had heard more than enough. He slid two *shuriken* from his jacket pocket and held them ready in his left hand while, with his right, he flung the door open.

Jug was standing in the doorway that led to the bedroom.

109

He was naked, his genitals and thighs covered with dried blood. He was not in a position to reach Ki quickly, but Slip was an immediate threat; he was dressed and walking across the big silkdraped chamber toward Ki. The arm Ki had dislocated was in a sling, but Slip's free hand had started for the butt of his holstered revolver when he saw Ki in the open door.

Ki loosed the *shuriken* that he'd slipped into his right hand the instant the door was open. With unerring accuracy, the thin steel blade spun in a bright, shimmering flash to Slip's throat and sank deep, its razor-sharp edges severing the outlaw's windpipe and jugular vein. Clawing at his throat with the hand that had started for his pistol, Slip took two more steps before crumpling silently to the floor.

When Jug saw his partner fall, he roared like a gored bull and lurched from the doorway, his arms going up, ready to grab Ki as soon as he could reach him.

Ki's reflexes were far faster than the big outlaw realized. While his first *shuriken* was still in the air, he'd taken the second into his throwing hand, and the steel blade was spinning toward Jug as the hardcase took his first step. Ki had not anticipated Jug's movement. The blade bit into Jug's collarbone instead of the vulnerable, unprotected flesh of his neck between his jaw and shoulder.

Jug roared with pain, but did not stop. Ki leaped forward and met Jug in the middle of the room. Jug reached for Ki, but Ki stopped short. His slippered toe took Jug in the crotch. The hulking hoodlum bent forward, an instinctive reaction that Ki had anticipated. Ki's fingers were already intertwined. He brought his clasped hands down in a swift, merciless blow to Jug's neck, at the base of the outlaw's skull, separating the vertebrae. Jug's momentum carried him one more step forward before he lurched forward and fell facedown, dead before he hit the floor.

Ki knew what he would find in the bedroom, but he went to the door and looked. Cheri was sprawled naked on the bed, in a pool of the blood that had spurted from a knife-slit in her throat. Her mouth was open in a ghastly grin, her eyes stared unseeingly ahead. The blood from her wound had left crimson bands like ribbons across the billows of her breasts.

Ki looked for only a few seconds before turning away. He stopped long enough to remove his *shuriken* from the bodies of Slip and Jug, then left the apartment and went down the stairs to the fenced yard. The fence was no obstacle. He made a short run, leaped to catch the top of the boards, and levered himself over. He landed on his feet in the street and saw Jessie walking toward him. Ki went to meet her.

★

Chapter 11

"Ki!" Jessie exclaimed as they got within easy speaking distance. "I was afraid you'd gotten into trouble when you didn't get back to Captain Tinker's last night." Her eyes took in Ki's dust-smeared vest and trousers. "From the way you look, I was right."

"There was a little trouble," he said. "It's over now."

"Have you had breakfast?"

Ki smiled. "I've been too busy to think about food."

"And you missed supper last night, I suppose?"

"I was busy last night, too."

"We'd better go back to Captain Tinker's, then," she suggested. "We can talk privately while we're walking, if you'd like to bring me up to date on what happened to you."

By a long-standing but unspoken agreement, there were few secrets between Jessie and Ki, though each of them realized there were areas of their personal lives that it would be better not to share. While both he and Jessie were usually aware of the events that took place in the other's private life, they did not discuss them in detail.

As he and Jessie turned and started walking toward the town square, Ki said, "We were right about the saloon being turned into a cartel headquarters, Jessie. But I'll tell you about that later. Last night—well, you remember the two hoodlums who'stopped us the day we got here?"

"Slip and Jug?"

"Yes. I was foolish enough to let them catch me off guard."

"And they held you prisoner?"

"Only for a few hours. I had been talking to a woman who I'm sure was the mistress of a man who holds a high position in the cartel. I'm reasonably sure he's responsible for getting the railroad started."

"You're talking about Prosser?"

"No, not Prosser. This man is in Virginia City, I'm sure, Jessie. His name is Frank Jeffers. I didn't get a chance to find out much more. If I'd asked too many questions so soon, she would have been suspicious. I decided not to act too eager."

"You met her in the saloon?"

Ki nodded. "We—we talked. She tried to persuade me to work for the man who sent her here to run the saloon. I'd hoped that through her I could learn who he is."

When Ki did not go on, Jessie frowned and asked, "Why do you say you hoped to, Ki? Isn't there a chance of learning anything more from her?"

"Slip and Jug killed her."

"How? By accident?"

"They'd have called it accidental, but it was murder."

"What happened?"

"Details aren't important, Jessie. Slip and Jug killed her before I could break out of the place where they'd put me. I had to kill both of them to get away."

Jessie was silent for a moment. When she saw that Ki was not going to add anything more, she said, "There must

113

be some way we can follow this lead you've uncovered, Ki."

"There is. If the barkeep at the saloon tells the sheriff I left with Cheri, it might be wise for me to stay out of sight for a few days. We can go follow that lead in Virginia City."

Jessie shook her head. "I've heard that since it's been rebuilt after that bad fire a few years ago, the silver mines are busier than ever. Ki, there are thirty thousand people there now. And how can you be sure that saloon girl gave you the man's real name? Finding him could take weeks."

Before Ki could tell Jessie that Cheri and the barkeep had given him enough clues to make their search easy, they'd reached the town square. On seeing the courthouse, she pointed to the building and went on quickly, "That's the first trouble spot we've got to clean up, Ki. Unless we can find records to prove that these people who live here have clear titles to their land, the railroad agent's going to dispossess them, and if he does, we're going to have a small war on our hands."

As they walked on, she told Ki what she'd encountered during the time they'd been apart: records missing from the courthouse, the two fires, Prosser's appearance and offers and threats, the meeting of Hidden Valley landowners that was to be held that night.

"You've been a lot busier than I have," Ki commented when Jessie had finished. "But think about going to Virginia City, Jessie. All that the cartel has here are fingers. What we can do there is strike at its arm."

"We'll talk about it later, Ki. Right now we've got enough to keep us busy here in Hidden Valley."

Jed Clemson was waiting when Jessie and Ki got back to the Tinker house. He told the Captain, "Dad and I got to talking after you left, and we made up a list of the men that ought to be at this meeting tonight. I'll take care of the ranchers down in the south valley, but there's more farms than he can get to in the time we've got. Can you give us a hand?"

"Jessie and I have got to go back to the courthouse and keep on looking for land deeds. Martha's fixed us some sandwiches so we won't lose time coming back here at noon."

"How about me, Grandpa?" Bobby asked. "I can take the buggy and—"

"Well, I guess you could, Bobby," the old man began, then he frowned and asked, "But are you sure you know enough about all this to explain it so they'd understand?"

Jessie broke in quickly, "Suppose Ki went with Bobby, Captain?" Her eyes flicked quickly to catch Ki's, and when he nodded approvingly, she added, "He could help Bobby explain."

"Now that's a shrewd idea," Tinker agreed. "We can cover all the ground that way. Let's leave them to get folks to the meeting, and the two of us will keep getting dust up our noses."

Examining the boxes of dusty records proved as unrewarding as it had been the day before. Noon came and passed, and Jessie and the Captain had still found nothing helpful. By midafternoon they'd gone through the boxes of old records, and were beginning on those of recent years.

"It looks to me like what we've done has just been wasted time, Jessie," Tinker said.

"It hasn't all been wasted," she replied. "Doesn't it seem odd to you that there are records of everything except land deeds in these boxes? I'd be willing to bet that somebody has gone through them and taken out every land deed they found."

Tinker frowned. "Now, that hadn't occurred to me. But if you're right, we'd be spitting into the wind if we kept on."

"There's another place where we should be able to find certified copies or originals of some of the deeds, though," Jessie went on. "And that's the bank. Unless it's different from others I know about, it would get copies of deeds when it lends money with land as a security. Surely some of the farmers and ranchers must have had to borrow during bad years."

"I'd guess most of 'em have," Tinker said. "Let's don't make too much more fuss here, then. We'll step across the street to the bank and see what Oscar Breyer has to say."

Breyer radiated cordiality when Jessie and the Captain first came in. Jessie recognized him as a model of small-town bankers. Smooth-shaven, the tracks of a combing still visible in his graying hair, Breyer looked and smelled like he was fresh from a barber's chair; even at that hour of the afternoon, a faint aroma of cologne and macassar-oil hairdressing still clung to him. His gray suit was brightened by an embroidered vest and a pearl stickpin in his wide cravat.

After settling Jessie and the Captain into chairs beside his ornately carved rolltop desk, the banker tugged the bottom tips of his embroidered waistcoat to remove the wrinkles that bulged when he sat down himself, and smiled at them benignly.

"It's always a pleasure to see you, Captain, and I've heard you mention the Starbuck name many times," Breyer said. "What can we do for you today?"

"We want some information, Oscar," Tinker said bluntly. "I guess you know the railroad's beginning to make trouble for some of the folks here who don't want to sell their good farmland for right-of-way?"

"I heard of the unfortunate events of last night, yes. But how does that concern you, Captain? Or Miss Starbuck?"

"Even if most of it happened before your time here, you'd know how I came by the land that I sold the people here in Hidden Valley," the Captain replied.

"Oh, of course," Breyer smiled. He waved his hand in an expansive gesture. "The Starbuck legend."

"It's not a legend," Jessie said quickly. "It happens to be true that my father gave the valley to Captain Tinker."

"I didn't mean any offense, Miss Starbuck," Breyer apologized. "I never doubted that the basic facts were true, but I know that stories of that kind are often colored by the years."

"This one isn't," she replied. "That's beside the point, though. Just how much do you know about the South Sierra Railway Company, Mr. Breyer?"

"They're among our depositors, of course," Breyer replied. "And I've seen their balance sheet, which I might add is very satisfactory for a business that hasn't really begun operating yet. Why do you ask, Miss Starbuck?"

Before Jessie could answer, the Captain said, "They're out buying right-of-way, but I guess you know that."

Breyer nodded. "I've been told that's their next step in building through the valley here."

"There's a lot of people don't want to sell to them, though. Farmers who'd have tracks running through their fields, cutting off their houses, things like that." The Captain stopped with a growing frown and shook his head. He went on, "There's been some talk about folks not having clear titles to their land, Oscar, people I sold the land to. Jessie and I, well, we've been trying to make sure the deeds are all in order."

"That's hardly a matter for the bank to be concerned with," Breyer said.

"We've been trying to find records at the courthouse," Jessie told the banker, "and haven't been able to. The Captain and I thought you might have some certified copies of deeds to land that was used as security for loans."

"I'm sure we do," Breyer replied. "But I don't see what the connection is between our loan records and the railroad."

"We were hoping you'd let us have copies of whatever deeds you might have in your files," Captain Tinker explained. "It'd help folks to know they've got a clear title to any land the railroad might be interested in, if the question should come up."

"Even if we did have copies of deeds in our loan files, it would be highly improper for us to give them to you,

117

Captain Tinker," Breyer said. "Those are confidential bank records."

"I'm sure any of your depositors who might have deeds filed with you will be glad to give you permission to let us have the copies we want," Jessie told the banker.

"That wouldn't make any difference, Miss Starbuck," Breyer said. "No bank will open its confidential files to anyone except a state or federal examiner."

"Suppose the people these files concern come in and ask for their deeds, Oscar?" The Captain asked. "Wouldn't you let them have copies of their deeds?"

"No, we wouldn't, Captain Tinker," Breyer replied. "Once a confidential file is established, it's bank property."

"Dammit, man, these people are your customers! Don't you feel like they've got some rights?" Tinker exclaimed.

"Oh, certainly they do," Breyer agreed. "But they don't have a right to any records that are the bank's property."

Jessie decided the time had come for a showdown. She said, "Mr. Breyer, you seem to be determined to put your bank's rules ahead of the interests of your depositors. As the Captain said, we need facts to help the people in Hidden Valley keep the railroad from stealing the land they've bought and paid for."

Breyer frowned. "Isn't 'stealing' much too harsh a word? As I understand it, the railroad is offering to pay very generously for the land it needs."

"It's also threatening to take land by force if the owners refuse to sell to them," she said coldly. "I'd hardly call that generous, Mr. Breyer."

"I haven't heard of any such threats, Miss Starbuck," the banker frowned. "Isn't it possible that you and Captain Tinker have been deceived by malicious gossip spread by troublemakers?"

"I heard the threats myself," Jessie answered. "They were made by Mr. Prosser. You're acquainted with him, I'm sure."

"Yes, of course. But I can't believe Karl would do anything like that," Breyer replied.

"I'm not accustomed to being called a liar, Mr. Breyer," Jessie said icily. She stood up. "If that's your attitude, Captain Tinker and I are wasting our time even talking to you."

Breyer was on his feet instantly. "Now please, Miss Starbuck! I made an unfortunate choice of words! I had no intention of implying that you weren't being truthful! Please accept my apologies and let's continue our conversation."

Captain Tinker said, "I'm sure Oscar didn't mean to insult you, Jessie. Why don't we—"

When she chose to do so, Jessie could be as haughty as any titled aristocrat. She kept her face frozen and matched it with the coldness of her voice. "It's obvious that Mr. Breyer is more interested in a group of rapacious scoundrels than he is in the welfare of the farmers and ranchers who support his bank, Captain Tinker. And I don't wish to spend a minute longer talking to a man who has called me a liar. You stay if you like. I won't."

Jessie started walking toward the door, Breyer following her, Jessie still ignoring his apologies. The Captain watched for a moment, then picked up his hat and joined them.

Breyer was still talking when they reached the door and Jessie left the bank. Captain Tinker sighed, and joined her on the sidewalk outside. Jessie started walking briskly toward the Tinker residence, the Captain vainly trying to keep up with her, but always a step or two behind. Jessie slowed her brisk pace, and as he came abreast of her and she turned to face him, Tinker was surprised to see her grinning.

"Do you think my imitation of an empty-headed society woman was good enough to fool Breyer?" she asked.

"You were just putting on all that high-hat business?" he asked when he'd recovered from his surprise.

"Have you ever seen me act that way before, Captain?"

"I can't say I have, Jessie. And it took me in, all right.

119

All I could think of was that Alex wouldn't have liked it a bit if he'd been here to see you. But why'd you do it?"

"Because I wanted him to think I'm a vain, snobbish fool who isn't capable of causing a great deal of trouble. I'm sure your friend Breyer will spread the word where that kind of report will help us the most."

"Don't call Oscar Breyer a friend of mine any longer. Not after what he just did."

"If we knew the truth, I think we'd find that Karl Prosser has been working very hard to develop a friendship with Mr. Breyer," Jessie said soberly. "Don't underestimate the cartel's agents. They have a way of corrupting men and still leaving their victims with the belief that they're honest."

"Are you saying Oscar's in cahoots with Prosser, Jessie?"

"I won't say yes, because I don't know," she said. "But I intend to find out a lot more about Mr. Breyer 'and his bank as soon as I have the time."

"How'll you go about finding out a thing like that, Jessie?" the Captain frowned.

"You know that my father had a lot of business interests here in the West. He did all his banking at the First California Bank in San Francisco, and I didn't change anything. I know they can give us all the information we need about Breyer," Jessie replied. She did not add that among the other Starbuck enterprises she'd inherited was a controlling interest in the bank. "Banks may have secrets from the public, but they don't have any among themselves."

Tinker chuckled. "You sure sound like Alex used to, Jessie. If he was here today, he'd be right proud of you."

"Thank you, Captain. When I run up against a problem that I can't seem to solve, I always ask myself what Father would have done; and usually that solves my problem."

They walked on in silence for a few moments, then Jessie said, "We can't really afford to regret the past, can we? There isn't any way we can change it."

"No. But there's sure a lot of things we'd change if we could. Like that bunch of crooks that meddled with the

120

deeds. If we hadn't elected them..." The Captain shook his head. "You know, Jessie, it ought to be possible for folks to change a mistake like that."

They'd taken a few more steps before Jessie stopped short, put her hand on her companion's arm, and said, "I think you just found the answer we need, Captain."

"If I did, I sure didn't know it. What'd I say?"

"Never mind that right now." Jessie's eyes were sparkling. "Is there a lawyer here in the valley?"

"Not a one except the county judge, and he's away. Why?"

"I want a copy of the territorial constitution."

"Wait now," Tinker frowned. "Ed Pashke's boy was studying to be a lawyer till last year, when he decided it'd take him too long to learn what he'd have to. Likely he'd have a copy."

"Where does he live?"

"Right up the street from my house. Why?"

"Let's go see if he has."

"What about the land deeds?"

"They can wait."

"Jessie, maybe you better tell me what kind of scheme you're hatching out," Tinker said.

"I'll tell you as we go. And if I'm right, we'll do some planning about that meeting we're going to have tonight. I think we might be able to tell these Hidden Valley folks what they can do to end the ugly situation the South Sierra Railway Company seems determined to create."

Chapter 12

Outside Captain Tinker's barn, waiting until they were sure there would be no more Hidden Valley residents arriving to join the crowd that had already gathered inside, the Captain, Jessie, Ki, and Jed Clemson stood talking.

"Some of those men in there look mean and mad, Jessie," the old seaman said. "Do you think we ought to go further than we decided we would, and tell them more?"

"No," she replied promptly. "Let's stick to our plan. Tell them everything we're sure is true. We can't tell them what we only suspect, things we know but can't prove yet."

"I'd feel like telling them our suspicions too, but I know that whatever we say in there, Prosser and Breyer and the rest of the railroad bunch are going to hear about it before the sun's over the yardarm tomorrow," the Captain said.

"They already know more than we do about their own plans," Ki pointed out. "Jessie's right, Captain. We should not let them know what we suspect."

Jed Clemson volunteered, "When I was out today spreading the word about the meeting, I found out that most of the valley folks know about the fires, but not much else. They haven't fitted all of it together the way you and Jessie and Ki have, Captain."

"There's one thing we shouldn't mention," Jessie said. "I don't suppose there'll be anyone here tonight who's ever heard of the cartel, or even suspects that such a thing exists."

"Well, I sure don't know a thing about it," Jed told her. "I didn't ask questions when I heard you mention it before, Jessie, but maybe you'd better tell me what you're talking about."

"We don't have time to do that now, Jed," Jessie said. "If you'll take my word and the Captain's that it's something that isn't good for Hidden Valley, I'll promise to explain later."

Tinker added quickly, "Jessie's right, Jed. You've got my word on what she's going to tell you later, too."

"I'd take either one of you on trust," Jed smiled. "When you both say the same thing, I figure I'd just better listen."

"Let's start the meeting, then," the Captain said. "All those people have to get up early tomorrow, and I've got a notion we're going to be here longer than we expect to be."

They went into the barn. To make room, the Captain had left his buggy outside, but the clear area in front of the stalls was so crowded that some of the younger and more agile of the men had climbed up into the hayloft, and a few had even shinnied out on the rafters. Jessie saw the eyes of the men focused on her curiously, and noticed that she was the only woman in the barn. Captain Tinker banged on a tin pail with the buckle of a harness strap to quiet the noisy buzz of talk.

"I don't suppose I need to waste your time telling you why we're here," he began. "Some of us know better than others what happened last night to Jethro and Rose Garvey, and Alice and Henry Clemson and their family. What we're

123

here for is to keep the same thing from happening to anybody else."

"We know what's been going on," a man called from the back of the crowd. "Let's cut the talk short and get the necktie party started!"

A half-dozen shouts of approval sounded. The captain held up his hands to silence them. He went on, "We didn't come here to set ourselves up as vigilantes. Nobody's been killed, and if we do the right thing here tonight, nobody's likely to be. We've got laws to go by, and the best thing we can do is use them."

"You better tell that to Prosser and the railroad bunch," a man in the front of the group said. "They're the ones that're breaking the law, not us."

"That's right!" the man standing next to the speaker added. "Nevada Territory ain't the best place in the country to talk about laws, Cap'n Bob. I guess we got enough laws, but nobody pays much attention to them."

"Especially the railroad," his companion added quickly.

Raising his voice over the murmur of approval that swept the crowd, the Captain said, "Now before I go on and tell you what we've found out, and what all of us need to do to hold onto what we've got, I'm asking you to keep quiet until I finish. There'll be plenty of time left for all of you to have a say when I get through." Leaning on his cane, he waited for the men to grow quiet, and went on, "I guess by now you know who the lady in back of me is. If you don't, she's Jessie Starbuck. It was her father gave me the land I sold you here in Hidden Valley."

"We know about Miss Starbuck and her daddy," someone called from the rafters. "Get on with what you got to say!"

"I will if you'll just let me!" the old man snapped tartly. When the buzz of talk died, he said, "Jessie and I have been going through the courthouse records the last few days, and we found out that somebody's done a lot of dirty work. All the land deeds you men filed are gone, and the record books

124

have been cut up. Even the deed I got for all of Hidden Valley's missing."

"Hell, that means we ain't nothing but squatters on land we bought and paid for!" an angry voice called.

The Captain's voice cut through the buzz that followed. "That's true! But even if the law calls you squatters, you've still got rights, and one of 'em is to hold the land you claim until a court can pass judgment on what kind of title you have."

"What'll we do when the railroad burns our houses and barns? Where are we gonna live while we try to hang on?" the man who'd suggested a lynching shouted above the hum of angry voices. "I say we go find that bastard Prosser and string him up!"

When only a few scattered voices rose in support of the proposal, Captain Tinker said quietly, "If we got rid of Prosser, the railroad would just send somebody else to do the same thing he's doing. Whatever we do has to be legal, or we're worse than the railroad is."

"They started this fight," one of the men said. "We didn't ask them to come in here with their damned tracks!"

"That's right!" another angry voice seconded. "They begun it, but I say let's us finish it!"

This time the voices raised in support of fighting were more numerous than before. Jessie decided to take a hand. She stepped up beside the Captain.

"Please!" she called. "Please listen to Captain Tinker! He has a plan to keep the railroad from robbing you without anybody getting hurt or killed!"

Jessie couldn't tell whether the men calmed down because of their interest in what she'd said, or because she was a woman. Listening to the mixture of rumbling voices die away, though, she was glad she'd refused to be the one to explain the plan they'd worked out and had insisted that the Captain do so.

"Let's go back to how all this got started," the old seaman

began. "But first I want to be sure everybody understands what's been going on."

"We know what's been going on, Cap'n Bob!" a man in the center of the group called out. "That damn railroad's started burning our houses so we won't be in shape to fight back when they take our land away from us, because we can't prove we bought it!"

"That's just half of it," Tinker said, raising his voice to be heard above the approving chorus that rose from the men. "The railroad's at the bottom of it, but how about the men you elected to look after the courthouse for you? Zeke Carter and Ed Kinsell and the judge? Didn't it ever occur to you that they sold you out?"

"Sure, but what can we do about that?" someone asked.

Another voice called, "We elected 'em for four years, and they still got two years to go!"

"If you can vote them into office, you can vote them out!" the Captain said loudly. "It's what's called a recall election." He held up the slim book that he and Jessie had borrowed earlier from the erstwhile law student. "It's right here in black and white, and I'll guarantee it'll be legal and binding. And while you're voting them out, you can elect men the railroad can't buy!"

"I say it's better to just string 'em up!" the lynching advocate shouted. "It's easier, and it'll save a lot of time!"

"Shut up!" a voice from the rafters commanded loudly. "If we'd wanted you to run things, we'd of asked you to! Listen to what Cap'n Bob says!"

After the echoes of approving shouts had died away, Tinker said, "All right. Now we might have to do this all over again to make it legal, but how many of you vote to throw out the men who're running the courthouse now?"

A roar of assenting voices filled the barn.

"Looks like we just voted ourselves a recall election," the Captain announced when the din had died away. "Now, then. Since you folks voted to toss out all the county of-

126

ficials, anybody who wants to put his name up to run for county clerk and sheriff and judge can sing out."

"How about it if we don't want to run ourselves, Cap'n Bob?" a man in the front of the crowd asked. "Is it all right if we put somebody else's name in the hat?"

"As long as you can guarantee he'll take whatever job he's elected to," Tinker replied.

"Then I'm nominating you to be the new county judge, and you better not say no!"

Captain Tinker hesitated for only a moment, then said, "If I take the job, it wouldn't be for long. I'd aim to resign from it as soon as this railroad mess is cleaned up."

"If you hogtie the railroad, that's all we ask you to do," replied the man who'd made the nomination.

"How about Paul Rogers for county clerk?" Jed asked. "We know he can read and write, and he'll keep things honest."

"Anybody got another name to put up?" Tinker asked. When no one spoke, he went on, "All right, now we need a sheriff."

Jethro Garvey spoke almost before the Captain had finished. "I say we can't do better'n Jed Clemson! He seen what happened to me, and the same thing almost happened to his folks! If he can't stop the fire-setting, nobody can!"

"Wait a minute!" a man from the haymow called. "Jed's got his hands full helping his folks on the farm and working for me on the ranch!"

"Then you take the job, Blaine Abel! You got enough hands on your place so you can spare the time!" Garvey shot back.

A few cries of approval and some applause followed the nomination. Tinker asked, "Well, Blaine, how about it?"

"If you men want me, I'll take it on," the rancher agreed.

His answer was a roar of approval from the crowd.

"Anybody got anything else to say?" Captain Tinker asked.

"Just tell us what we do now!" someone suggested.

"Before we can do anything else, we'll have to send somebody to Carson City and get the governor to sign some papers that'll make what we've done legal," Tinker replied. "And since you've elected me judge, I guess that's my job. But I don't look for any trouble. I've known Governor Kinkead for a long time. He's a good man, and he doesn't like crooks."

"You reckon we've done enough for tonight, then, Cap'n Bob?" a man in the crowd called.

"I'd say we've done a right good job," Tinker answered. "But we're still a ways from finishing it. The big job's going to be when we finish cleaning house and tackle the railroad."

"If we're through, I'm going home to bed," another of the men announced. "I got a day's work ahead of me tomorrow!"

In a surprisingly short time, the crowd broke up. Captain Tinker waited until it had thinned out before he hobbled to the wall to extinguish the nearest of the lanterns that had provided light for the meeting. Ki saw that the old seaman was moving slowly, leaning heavily on his cane, and hurried to help.

"Let me finish taking care of the lanterns, Captain," he said. "You're tired. Go on in the house and sit down."

"Thanks, Ki. This damn dickety leg of mine kicks up when I use it as much as I've had to lately," Tinker replied.

Just outside the barn door, Paul Rogers and Blaine Abel had stopped to talk with three or four of the men who'd remained behind. Jessie, waiting for Ki and the Captain, stood a few feet away, talking to Jed Clemson and his father.

"If you've got a minute, Captain, maybe you'd like to hear what these fellows have to say," Abel called.

Captain Tinker started walking toward the group just as the sharp crack of a rifle shot shattered the night's quiet.

Jessie was turning to join the Captain, when out of the corner of her eye she glimpsed the red spurt of a muzzle

128

blast, high above the ground. Her hand moved by instinct toward her hip before she remembered she hadn't thought it necessary to wear her pistol to the meeting.

While the old seaman's body was still jerking and whirling from the impact of the rifle slug, Jessie saw Jed Clemson and Blaine Abel drawing their revolvers, their heads swiveling as they searched for the source of the shot.

"On the roof of the barn next door!" she called to them, pointing. "There!"

Jed and Abel, unable to pierce the night's blackness with their eyes, started running toward the spot Jessie had indicated.

Jessie hurried on to Captain Tinker, who by this time had crumpled to the ground. Jessie dropped on her knees beside him.

Boot heels scrabbled harshly on the barn's shingles. Jed and Abel had not yet reached the fence that divided the Tinker yard from the barn where the rifleman had stationed himself. Before they could scale the fence, the thudding of hoofbeats told them the sniper was escaping.

Captain Tinker groaned and stirred and tried to raise himself, but fell back heavily. He said to Jessie through clenched teeth, "I forgot how a bullet hurts a man! Damn painful, Jessie!"

Supporting the old seaman with her arm, Jessie asked, "Where were you hit?"

"Leg. It's my good leg, too! If the son of a bitch had to shoot me, why in hell didn't he pick the one that's bad already?"

Holstering their weapons, knowing that pursuit was useless, Jed and Abel came up to Jessie and the captain. The back door of the house slammed as Martha came running out and knelt next to the Captain and Jessie.

"Oh, Captain!" she moaned. "How bad is it?"

"Don't fret, Martha," Tinker replied. "I've been hurt a lot worse. It's just my leg."

"We'll get him inside," Abel said.

Carrying the Captain between them, the two men started for the house. Martha went ahead to open the door, and Jessie followed, carrying the old man's cane. Jed and Abel edged through the kitchen with the Captain and headed toward the door leading to the bedrooms.

"Haul in!" Captain Tinker commanded. "Put me down in that chair over there. Martha won't like it if I go dripping blood on her nice clean carpets!"

"You'd better do what he says," Martha told them. "I've got hot water and everything else I need right at hand in here, anyhow. And the way he's cutting up, he's not bad hurt."

"Mind your language, Martha," the Captain chided. "I'm hurt bad enough, but I've been shot before, a lot worse than this."

Martha and Jessie tended to Tinker, slitting his trouser leg and the clinging, bloodstained leg of his balbriggans to expose the wound. The bullet had passed through his upper thigh, missing the bone, making two neat holes that were seeping a trickle of blood.

"Humph!" the captain grunted, craning his neck to inspect the wound. "I guess I'm lucky. Prosser or Breyer or whoever sent that fellow picked a damned bad shot."

"Oscar Breyer?" Abel asked, his voice rising in surprise. "What's he got to do with it?"

"Looks like he's in with the railroad rascals too," Tinker said. "There's some things Jessie and I found out today that we haven't had time to tell anybody."

"If Oscar's in with the railroad gang, I don't want my money in his damned bank!" the rancher said angrily.

"Just reef your sails, Blaine," the Captain told him. "All we've got now is suspicions. But Jessie's going to find out. She says she can get one of the banks in San Francisco to look into what Breyer's doing."

Martha knelt beside the chair and began washing the Captain's thigh with hot water. He winced as the washcloth rubbed over the muscle, and winced more when Martha

130

took a smaller pan containing a reddish liquid and began trickling it slowly over the wound.

Through gritted teeth, he said, "That hurts worse than the bullet did, Martha. You sure you didn't use too much permanganate in the water?"

"I'm sure," she answered. "Now keep still. And talk to somebody else while I finish cleaning up your leg and get a bandage on it."

Blaine Abel said to the Captain, "I might not be the legal sheriff yet, but I'm going to get the ranchers together, and all of us will put some of our hands out patrolling, just to let everybody know we're starting to fight back."

"That's a fine idea, Blaine," Tinker nodded. He looked at Jessie. "I guess you're going to have to talk to the governor for me, but I'll write him a letter that'll tell him what's been happening here. I was looking forward to seeing John, too. We just had one visit after he got back from Alaska a few years ago, then he got all wound up in politics and didn't have time."

"Don't worry, Captain," Jessie replied. "Even though I've never met him, if Governor Kinkead and Alex were as close friends as you say, I don't think Ki and I will have any trouble."

Ki came in, carrying a lantern. He arrived in time to hear Jessie mention his name, and stopped inside the door. "Am I missing something?" he asked. "Are we going somewhere, Jessie?"

"You and Bobby got back so late that I didn't have time to talk with you before the meeting, Ki," she answered. "But while you were gone, Captain Tinker and I decided that the three of us need to go to Carson City and talk to Governor Kinkead."

"Have you thought how close Virginia City is to Carson City, Jessie?" Ki asked. "It's only a half-day's ride. And we'd be foolish not to go and follow the lead I uncovered."

"Don't worry. We'll be going there too."

"I'm going to give you some advice now, Jessie," Tinker

131

said. "I know you and Ki travel together a lot, and taking a strange trail won't bother you. But the shortest way to Carson City goes through the mountains, and it's not safe for anybody who doesn't know it."

"We'll take the marked trail, then," Jessie said.

Tinker shook his head. "That's a four-day ride, Jessie, up the old Bidwell Trail north, and back south over the Pony Express road. The short way through the mountains is rough, but it cuts your trip down by two days. Since I can't go with you, my advice is to take along somebody else who knows that back trail."

Jessie said, "Your advice sounds good, Captain. Who do you think should go with us?"

"I had Jed in mind." The captain looked at Blaine Abel. "Can you spare him for a few days, Blaine? And let us have horses for Jessie and Ki?"

"Looks like I'd better, if you think they'll need him," the rancher replied. "And I've got saddle horses on the spread that don't get enough riding, this time of year." Turning to Jed, he asked, "Any reason why you wouldn't want to go?"

"Not a one, as long as it's all right with you."

"The Captain and I were planning to leave the day after tomorrow, about daybreak," Jessie told Jed. "Can you be ready in time?"

"Sure thing. That'll give me time to ride down to the ranch and get my rifle and saddlebags, and cut out a couple of horses for you and Ki."

"It's all settled, then," the Captain said. "And when you get back here, we'll be set to get rid of the railroad outlaws once and for all!"

★

Chapter 13

When they set out with Jed for Carson City, Jessie and Ki discovered before the end of the first day of their trip that Captain Tinker had not exaggerated when he warned them the trail was unsafe for strangers.

After leaving Hidden Valley by the north pass, an hour's ride brought them to the rough grade that had been cut for the railroad, but they had ridden beside it for less than a mile when Jed turned his horse westward. Through the clear morning air, which made it seem only a few miles away, the eastern face of the Sierra Nevadas reared like a massive wall, towering in one abrupt thrust above the lesser mountains through which the three would travel.

Jessie and Ki followed Jed over a well-marked trail through a wide, shallow valley. They made fast progress, and soon after the sun slid down to afternoon, they passed through what was left of the little town of Ludwig, the result and quickly the victim of a short-lived mining boom. The un-

133

paved street along which they rode was bordered on both sides with abandoned buildings and houses. Though here and there they saw one that still looked occupied, they saw neither human nor animal as they made their way through the remains of the town.

With more than half of the first day of their two-day ride now behind them, Jessie and Ki began to wonder why Captain Tinker had told them their trip would be a hard one. They soon received an answer to their unspoken question. After leaving Ludwig, the trail grew progressively worse. Time after time, Jed led them into canyons along trails that were no more than a few scratches made by prospectors, trails that both Jessie and Ki knew they'd have ignored, if they had been alone.

Often now, the trails dwindled and almost vanished as they wove through narrow, serpentine canyons on ledges very little wider than the horses' hooves. At times the ledges along which they squeezed were so narrow that their legs brushed the canyon wall. From some of these, a rider could have touched the rocky canyon wall with one hand and dropped a stone straight down for a half-mile with the other, without extending either arm full length.

"I see now why the Captain didn't want us to try this trail without you, Jed," Jessie said as they dismounted for the night at a spot Jed had picked, where the ground was almost level and the slope less precipitous than most.

Prompted by Jessie's question, Ki asked, "Is it like this all the rest of the way to Carson City?"

"No. We're close to being through the worst of it," Jed replied. "By noon tomorrow we'll be through these hills and on the flats. Then we'll make better time. I'll have us in Carson City by sun down tomorrow evening."

Though the sun had set the next day when they reached Carson City, Jessie and Ki agreed that Jed had kept his word. They'd passed through the foothill spur before noon and crossed a series of wide, sagebrush-dotted valleys; then, as they mounted to the rim of a shallow, saucerlike depression, the town suddenly came into sight on their left.

"We're there," Jed announced. "That's Carson City."

Long before they could make out details of other buildings and houses, they saw the slim dome of Nevada Territory's capitol rising from the saucer's rim. The dome's silver coating was a light-washed blue in the early, uneven twilight. While the capitol dome was bathed in brightness even in the fading day, the slope beyond it was in the shadow of the Sierras. Houses stood in ranks almost to the top of the rise, and lighted windows were already showing in some of them.

Jessie and Ki moved up to ride abreast of Jed as the trail became a street lined with small, neat, gingerbread-trimmed houses. They turned into the main street and rode toward the capitol's dome. After they'd passed the square, squat façade of the U.S. Mint, houses gave way to a scattering of stores, small office buildings, and saloons. Almost directly across from the capitol, Jed led them to the rear of a rambling stone building set back from the street, pulled up beside a row of carriages that stood in front of a huge barn, and swung out of his saddle.

"Even if it's past sunset, it's still daylight," he said. "And just like I promised you, we're at the Ormsby House. It might not look like much, but the beds are clean and soft, and they set a real good table."

"I'm hungry enough after two days of trail rations," Jessie said. "But I saw a lot of lights in the windows of the capitol building. Even if it's getting late, I wonder if the governor might still be in his office."

"If you and Jed are willing to wait for supper, I am too," Ki told her. "Let's go across the street and find out."

"Why don't you and Ki go, Jessie?" Jed suggested. "Let me stay here, I'll see the horses are tended and get our rooms."

"If you don't mind, Jed," Jessie replied. "Perhaps if Governor Kinkead hasn't gone home, he'd be willing to talk to us now. It might even be possible to finish our

135

business with him this evening and get an early start tomorrow for Virginia City."

Governor Kinkead was in his office, and when Jessie sent her name in to him by the clerk who guarded the inner door, Kinkead himself came out to greet her. He took both her hands and held them between his palms while he gazed into her green eyes.

"Alex Starbuck's daughter!" he exclaimed. "And I can see the resemblance, Jessie—I'm going to call you Jessie, because I feel like I'm your uncle. Your father was as close to me as any of my brothers ever were."

"I'd like that, Governor," Jessie replied. She responded at once to the friendliness radiating from the bearded face of the tall, sturdy man standing in front of her. The feeling of the governor's palms on her hands comforted her; they had the firmness that told of calluses formed by work and not yet gone soft, the hands of a man of action. She nodded in Ki's direction and said, "This is Ki. He was my father's friend and companion for years, and now he's mine."

The governor nodded, releasing Jessie's hands to shake Ki's. "If you were Alex's friend, Ki, consider me yours."

"Thank you, Governor," Ki said. "Mr. Starbuck spoke of you often during the years I was with him. I remember that once he was getting ready to go to Alaska to visit you, but some urgent business problem made him postpone the trip."

"I'm deeply indebted to Alex," Kinkead said. "He used his influence in Washington to help those of us up there who finally persuaded Seward to buy Alaska from Russia back in '67."

"That was before I was old enough to understand anything about my father's business," Jessie said.

"Even before that, your father had helped me, Jessie," the governor went on. "When I was first setting up my business in San Francisco in '54, he did more than any other man would've done for a ragged stranger." His face grew

136

sober. "It's tragic that a few scoundrels should rob the world of a man with his vision and foresight."

"Father's death wasn't the work of just a few scoundrels," Jessie said quietly. "That's the reason I'm here. I hope you're not too busy to talk for a few minutes, not necessarily now, but when you finish whatever work is keeping you here so late—"

Kinkead interrupted her. "We can talk right now, Jessie. The legislature's having a night session, and all I have to do is wait. We may be interrupted long enough for me to sign my name, that's all. Let's go in my office, where we can talk privately."

When Jessie and Ki had settled into the big horsehair-padded armchairs that stood in front of Kinkead's desk, the governor said, "I never enjoy night legislative sessions. When I miss my supper—" He stopped and looked at Jessie and Ki. "Have you had yours, by the way?"

"No," Jessie replied. "We saw the lights in here and I was so anxious to see you that Ki and I came over at once."

"That means you're stopping at the Ormsby House, then," Kinkead said. "I was just about to send my clerk across the street to order my supper. The Ormsby House is used to sending me meals when I can't leave at noon, and when I'm working late. Suppose you and Ki have dinner with me here in the office?"

"We'd enjoy it," Jessie answered after a quick look at Ki. "There's a young man with us, but I'm sure Ki will go over and explain to him."

"Include him in my invitation, if you like," the governor suggested. "I assume he's with you because he has a part in the matter that's brought you here."

"Yes, he does."

Ki stood up. "I'll go tell Jed, then."

After Ki had gone, Kinkead was silent for a moment, looking at Jessie. Finally he said, "You're very like your father, you know. And I feel badly about something, Jessie.

137

Perhaps if I tell you this now, it'll ease my feelings. Do you mind?"

"Do go ahead," she invited.

"I didn't learn of your father's murder until after I got back from Alaska, Jessie. And I didn't realize that you were carrying on what he'd created. I should've written you, but business and politics combined have a way of keeping a man busy day and night. You'll overlook my negligence, I hope."

"Of course I will, Governor! I'm just glad I've gotten to meet you. And while I'm not involved in politics, trying to preserve what Father left me has kept me busy too."

"That's what's brought you here, then? I know that Alex had some very substantial land holdings here in Nevada Territory. If I recall correctly, they were in Hidden Valley, but I thought he'd passed all that land on to Captain Bob Tinker."

Jessie nodded. "He did. And I have a letter from Captain Tinker to give you, about the trouble the people are having in Hidden Valley."

Kinkead frowned. "I haven't heard of any trouble there."

"It's just begun," Jessie said. "Until a few days ago, the people there didn't understand what was happening, and most of them still don't. But the cause of the trouble goes back to the days when Father bought the valley land, not because he needed it, but because he wanted to keep—" She stopped and frowned, then asked, "Governor Kinkead, did Father ever mention that he'd been invited to become a member of a large European cartel?"

"He mentioned the offer, but told me he'd refused them."

"Oh, yes, he refused. But they'd told him too much about their schemes and the way they operate when they were trying to persuade him to join them." Jessie was silent for a moment, holding her emotions firmly in check. Then she went on, "You said a few minutes ago that a few scoundrels murdered my father. That covers the bare facts, but the

138

whole truth is that the killers were a gang sent by the cartel to murder him."

"And the cartel is trying to get a foothold now, here in Nevada Territory?"

"I'm sure they already have a foothold, or at least a toehold," Jessie replied quietly. "What they're trying to do now is to expand their power and influence through a new railroad. They call it the South Sierra Railway Company, and they must have been planning it for years."

Kinkead frowned. "I know about the railroad, of course. It was chartered by one of my predecessors, so I'm not really too familiar with it, but it seems to me that it was chartered only two or three years ago."

"I'm sure that's right. But when Father bought the Hidden Valley land, the cartel was trying to buy it even then, and he got it away from them. Now they're after it again for their railroad, and they're starting—well, I suppose it's something close to a small war to get their hands on the valley."

For a moment the governor looked at Jessie, his high forehead furrowed thoughtfully. Then he said, "If anybody but you had come to me with this story, Jessie, I wouldn't have believed it. But when I look at you and see the reflection of your father in your eyes, I know that what you've told me is true. Now tell me what I can do to help."

During the trip, there'd been plenty of time for Jessie to organize the sequence of events that had taken place in Hidden Valley, and to be sure her interpretation of their significance would be logical and straightforward. Speaking rapidly, she told Kinkead of Bobby's visit to the Circle Star, and the effort to kill Ki and herself on their trip to the valley. She'd reached the episode of Ki's capture and what he'd learned from Cheri when Ki returned with Jed.

When Jessie resumed her story after they'd settled down, she made a point of bringing Jed into her narration, asking him to speak for the Hidden Valley farmers and ranchers.

139

Jed had been anticipating meeting the governor too, and his remarks were as terse and to the point as Jessie's had been. Their story was still a long one, though. When they'd finished it, Kinkead leaned back in his chair, an angry frown on his face.

"I won't say that what you've told me is a shock, Jessie," he began. "I've rubbed up against a lot of unscrupulous men in my lifetime. As a boy back in Pennsylvania, I learned there were men who'd stop at nothing to get what they wanted. Since then, I've been in business in Ohio and Utah, before I moved to San Francisco and then Alaska, and I've found it's the same all over. From what you've told me, this cartel is even worse than most. But there are some things I can do that will help you."

When Kinkead stopped, pulled a tablet of paper across the desk, and reached for a pen from the elaborate inkstand in front of him, Jed said, "Jessie told you a lot of things about that cartel outfit that I hadn't heard before. And right now the folks in Hidden Valley could sure use some help. Captain Bob was even thinking about asking you to call out the militia."

"I'm afraid our militia wouldn't be much help to you," the governor smiled. "It exists only on paper, Jed. Aside from a few war veterans, nobody's interested in military matters now."

"What do you plan to do, then, Governor?" Jessie asked.

"Several things. First I'll get your hasty recall election legalized. It takes a resolution by the legislature to authorize a recall election, Jessie, and the people in the valley will have to vote again, with proper printed ballots."

"There won't be any trouble getting them to do that," Jed said quickly. "The Captain figured we'd have to vote again to make things legal."

"Good," Kinkead said. "The next move I'll make is to have the legislature's Commerce Committee investigate the South Sierra Railway Company, with the intention of revoking their charter. That will take time, though. The election matter can be settled at once, at tomorrow's session. I don't know what I can do about the bank, though. The chairman of the Banking and Finance Committee is my chief political enemy, and—"

"Leave the bank to me," Jessie broke in. "As soon as I can send a telegram to San Francisco, I'll take care of that, and the territorial legislature won't have to be involved."

"You can use the wire here in my office," Kinkead offered. "Or when you get to Virginia City, you'll find a public telegraph there. In fact, thanks to Hearst and Mackay and Fair and their Combination, Virginia City had telegraph service five years before the capital of the territory did."

A knock sounded on the office door, and after a polite pause, Kinkead's clerk opened it wide enough to stick his head in. "I hate to disturb you, Governor," he said, "but the chairman and two members of the Appropriations Committee need to consult with you for a few minutes."

Jessie stood up, and Ki and Jed followed her example. She said, "I'll send my wire from Virginia City, Governor Kinkead. We'll be heading there early in the morning."

"But you'll stop and see me on your way back to Hidden Valley, I hope?" Kinkead asked. "There are still a lot of things I'd like to talk with you about."

"Of course we will!" Jessie assured him. "And I'll save my thanks until we see you again."

Walking across the street to the Ormsby House, Ki said, "We found a real friend just when we needed one, I'd say. The governor can do things that we'd never be able to do alone."

Jessie nodded, then smiled. "It's strange not to be fighting the cartel by ourselves, isn't it, Ki?"

Before Ki could answer, Jed said, "Don't forget I'm here too, Jessie. And the folks back in Hidden Valley are with us."

"I didn't intend to leave you and the others out," Jessie said. "But most of the time when Ki and I get into one of these open battles with the cartel, the people we're trying

141

to help aren't even aware that such a thing exists."

"You were going to tell me more about it," Jed reminded her as they entered the Ormsby House.

"And I will. But not now," Jessie replied. "We've had a long two days, and all of us need rest. We'll talk on the way to Virginia City tomorrow, Jed."

Jessie had not realized how very short the distance was from Carson City to Virginia City. They'd gotten up yawning from beds they'd found luxuriously soft after a night on the hard ground, and started out when the sun was just gilding the towering peaks of the Sierra Nevadas. Still tired, they'd talked very little. The sun was still low in the east and the cartel had not been mentioned when they came to the first rise in a cluster of cone-shaped hills, and sighted the first mines, marked by huge smokestack-topped buildings that rose above the shafts and housed big steam engines that provided power for the pumps and hoists.

"We're nearly there," Jed said. He pointed to the first and highest of the hills, and with the same gesture indicated the tall, ramshackle structure that clung high on its sloping side. Below the building, huge heaps of raw dirt covered the steep side of the mountain. Jed went on, "They call that Mount Davidson, and if I remember rightly, that mine's the Yellow Jacket. The town's just another couple of miles ahead."

Belatedly, Jessie remembered her promise and told Jed, "I'm sorry we haven't talked about the cartel, Jed. I thought we'd have a half-day of riding and plenty of time to talk. But I haven't forgotten, and we'll have time while we're here."

"I'm not in any hurry, Jessie," Jed replied. "Except I am a mite curious."

Ki said, "I'm not sure we'll be in Virginia City as long as you think we will, Jessie. With what we already know, it shouldn't take us too much time to turn up this Frank Jeffers."

"I hope you're right, Ki," she replied. "But we've both learned that finding someone when we don't want him to know we're looking for him can be a long job. And from what I've heard, Virginia City's as busy as an anthill and twice as crowded."

"We've got to get back to the valley as quick as we can," Jed reminded them. "The Captain will need the papers the governor promised us before he can do very much."

They passed the base of Mount Davidson and reached the end of the curve that the road made around its base. The wide, rutted thoroughfare stretched ahead of them, a wavering line on a wide, uptilted shelf that extended from the clump of hills. Perched precariously on the sides of each hill were one or two or sometimes three or four buildings similar to that which Jed had pointed out as the Yellow Jacket mine. Absorbed in looking at the mountainsides, Jessie and Ki did not notice that at some point the road had become a street until Jed reined in.

"C Street," he announced, pointing to the houses that clung precariously to the sides of the hills ahead. "And that's Virginia City."

★

Chapter 14

Jessie and Ki reined in their horses beside Jed. Though Jessie had traveled to many places, she had never beheld a scene like the one that lay before them.

A short distance ahead, C Street widened into a smoothly paved thoroughfare, and still farther ahead there were buildings stretching away from it on both sides. On the sharply sloped flank of the valley below the shelf, a score or more huge shafthead sheds stood, the tops of their smokestacks towering above the heads of the riders.

Wagons with teams of ten mules hitched to them were lined up on a narrow wagon road that wove its way from one of the mine buildings to the next, the wagons moving so slowly that they seemed to be standing still. Great piles of raw yellow lumber surrounded the sheds, and the steeply pitched ground that stretched beyond the lumber stacks was covered with heaps of fresh dirt tailings, their conical sides shimmering wetly.

While they sat looking at the sheds, the chugging of a locomotive and the sharp blast of its whistle almost underfoot set the horses dancing. The train had passed with a screeching of wheels on curving rails before they'd calmed the animals, and when Jessie looked down into the valley, she saw only the caboose disappearing around the curve in the shining tracks.

"I didn't know there was a railroad here," she frowned. "I suppose it only hauls materials between the mines, though."

"Oh, no," Jed said. "That's the Virginia & Truckee Railroad. It goes clear up into the mountains over across the California line. It hauls lumber for mine timbers from there and takes refined silver to Truckee, where it's loaded on the Central Pacific and sent on to San Francisco."

"It doesn't carry passengers, then?" she asked.

"Well, it does, only I've heard you've got to have a real strong stomach to ride it, or you'll get sick. They say the tracks from here to Truckee have got more crooks and curves than any railroad in the world. But it carries passengers to Truckee, and they get the CP from there on into San Francisco."

"I see," Jessie said thoughtfully. "Well, I have some business in San Francisco. I hadn't planned to go there myself, but if it's necessary, I know now that it's possible."

They rode on slowly, looking now at the town. The ground rose ahead of them, and being on horseback extended their field of vision so that they saw the town much like a map held at an angle to their eyes. Two steep hills that rose behind C Street, their peaks not quite a mile apart, defined the town as well as confining it. The bases of the hills extended almost to C Street, and the ledge or shelf along which the street ran was wide enough only for a single row of buildings that backed up to the dropoff above the shaft-head sheds. The rest of the town was crowded into the broad vee between the hills.

On the level shelf of the vee along which C Street ran,

the ground was covered with buildings standing wall to wall. Terraced streets had been cut at intervals up both steep sides of the valley, and houses faced these streets. Like the buildings on the strip of flat and relatively level land along which C Street ran, the houses on those streets were closely spaced, separated by no more than a yard or two. Few of the buildings were imposing. Almost all of them were simple single-story frame structures, though scattered here and there were a few houses built of brick, some of these two or even three stories high.

On the sloping sides of the canyon below C Street, beyond the shafthead structures and overpowered by the chutes and boxed-in runs for hoist cables, were other houses. Most of these were small and shabby, and some were little more than shanties. A majority of these had been built of boards, their surfaces now weatherbeaten, while those on the hillsides above the business section were freshly painted and appeared to be new.

That the structures along C Street and immediately behind it were business buildings could be seen at a glance, for some were two or three stories high at the front, though in many places the space between street and slope was barely enough to accommodate their foundations and the beginnings of their side walls. Level foundations for a few had been excavated from the hillsides, but for the most part the foundation lines of the long, narrow structures tapered upward from the street to conform with the rise of the slope, and at their backs the eaves were almost level with the slanting ground that rose above their roofs.

Even at that early-morning hour, C Street itself was like the anthill to which Jessie had compared the town earlier. There was little wheeled traffic; only a half-dozen buggies could be seen, and even fewer wagons, but the street was awash with men, some moving purposefully, the others strolling idly. Here and there the feathered plume of a wide-brimmed hat marked the passage of a woman, but these

146

could have been counted on the fingers of one hand, with the thumb left over.

They reined their horses to a walk when they reached the first of the pedestrians. Jessie had been looking at the town's buildings as well as at the crowd, and now she said, "So far, all I've seen is fleabag lodging houses and sleazy hotels. Surely there are some good hotels here, aren't there, Jed?"

Jed pointed ahead, to a massive red brick building that dominated the center of the town. It rose six stories, its façade punctuated with rows of windows capped by arched limestone lintels, and an elaborate pediment of the same white stone circling the walls below a mansard roof.

"That's the International Hotel," Jed said, as Jessie and Ki gazed at the imposing structure. "I never have stopped there, but I hear it's the best hotel between Denver and San Francisco."

"We'll find out if it is," Jessie told him. "Since we'll be here several days, we need a place for our headquarters where we can have meals served and talk privately. I'll get a suite, Jed, with a sitting room and separate bedrooms for each of us."

After a moment's hesitation, Jed said somewhat hesitantly, "I understand rooms there are right expensive, Jessie. I didn't bring much money with me—"

"Don't worry about that," Jessie replied. "Money isn't as important to me as having what we need for our job here. And I like to be comfortable, of course."

"Well, I'll pay my share, then," Jed insisted.

"We can talk about that later," Jessie said. "The first thing to do is to find out if the International has room for us."

When they went into the International Hotel, and Jessie gave her name to the desk clerk, a suite was made available without hesitation. The clerk may have had the Starbuck name impressed on the mental roster of the wealthy and

147

powerful that is carried in the minds of employees in luxury hotels; or, despite Jessie's travel-worn clothes, he may have recognized the calm assurance of authority with which she made her request.

Jessie glanced at the guest register when the desk clerk put it in front of her, and said, "I would prefer that my name not show in your register. Please oblige me by signing for the suite to show that it is occupied by Miss Johnson and party."

Without changing expression, the clerk nodded calmly, as though such requests were commonplace. He said, "Of course, Miss Johnson." He signed the register, turned it to show the entry to Jessie, and asked, "Are you traveling by carriage?"

Jessie shook her head. "By horseback. Our mounts are in front of the hotel."

"Very good, Miss Johnson. A bellboy will bring in your luggage and show you to your suite. I'll have a stableman take care of your horses."

When Jed entered the suite and saw its richly carved walnut furniture and ornate Oriental rugs, and through the open doors of the bedrooms saw the private bathrooms that adjoined each of them, his eyes widened, but he made no comment. Ki and Jessie paid little attention to their surroundings. They picked up their saddlebags and stood looking at the open bedroom doors.

Ki said, "You choose the room you want, Jessie. Jed and I will take the others."

"As far as I can tell, the bedrooms are identical," Jessie said. "Suppose I take the one in the center. As soon as I bathe and get into fresh clothes, we'll decide where to start."

"A good idea," Ki said. "The only thing lacking in the Ormsby House was enough bathtubs."

Before she reached the bedroom door, Jessie turned and said to Ki, "I intend to have a long, lazy soak, Ki. You and Jed will probably finish bathing before I do, so why don't you tell Jed what you learned from that saloon girl?

It'll help him to understand how important it was for us to come here to Virginia City."

Ki and Jed returned to the sitting room only a few moments apart. Ki had just settled into one of the brocade-upholstered easy chairs when Jed came in. He sat down in the chair nearest Ki and waited expectantly.

Ki asked, "How much do you know about what Cheri told me?"

Jed shook his head. "Not a thing. I guess Cheri's that saloon girl Jessie was talking about, but I don't recall hearing her name before. I stay pretty much away from saloons, Ki."

"I'd better start at the beginning, then."

As briefly as he could, Ki told Jed of his conversations with the barkeep and Cheri, and what he'd heard listening to the exchange between Slip and Jug after Cheri's death. He cut his narrative as short as possible, condensing and summarizing, omitting much detail. Jed's brow began furrowing while Ki talked, and when he'd heard the last of the details that Ki saw fit to include, his frown had deepened to a puzzled scowl.

"You killed both of them just like that?" Jed asked. "One of 'em carrying a pistol and the other one coming at you?" He shook his head. "I'm not saying I don't believe you, Ki, but—"

"I can only tell you what happened, Jed," Ki said quietly. "But when we have time, I will show you that I can throw two of my *shuriken* in less time that a man can draw a pistol."

Jed was still frowning. "The other thing I can't figure out is how you got this Cheri woman to tell you as much as she did."

"She was trying to enlist me into the cartel. She had to tell me about the man we came here to find, this Frank Jeffers."

"Now I haven't been around much, but I've got enough sense to know a woman's not going to talk all that much without a pretty good reason," Jed said. "You didn't come right out with it, but I know how women get softened up and like to say things they might not otherwise to a man who's just given 'em a good pronging." Ki did not take Jed's hint. After a moment, Jed asked, "Am I right about that, Ki? Go on and tell me. I promise I won't say a word to Jessie."

Ki said quietly, "Jessie already knows."

"She does?"

"Certainly."

"But I thought—" Jed stopped in confusion, stared at Ki for a moment, and went on, "I mean, I was sure—you and her traveling around together everywhere the way you do, I guess I just figured—"

"You figured wrong, Jed," Ki said. "I see that you don't understand how it is between Jessie and me."

"I guess I sure as hell don't!" Jed was now embarrassed as well as confused. "But I've put my foot deep enough in my mouth already. I don't aim to shove it down my throat any further."

"Don't feel embarrassed," Ki said. "It's easy to make such a mistake, and very hard for some people to understand what is really between Jessie and me."

"Why don't you try to tell me?"

"I'm not sure I can find the words I need." Ki frowned and thought for a moment. "When I came to this country, I knew no one except Alex Starbuck. My family had—well, my father was American, and my Japanese mother's family did not approve of my mixed blood. An outcast in my own country, I came here to the United States. Alex Starbuck had been a friend of my father's, and I went to him. He gave me work, and later I became his assistant. Jessie was a young girl when I first began working for her father. I watched her grow up, and when Alex was killed, she asked me to serve her as I had served Alex."

Ki paused, his eyes fixed unobtrusively on Jed. The young ranch hand was frowning as he tried to assimilate all

150

that Ki had said, and to guess at what had been left unspoken.

"I guess you and Jessie are sort of like a sister and brother, then," Jed frowned. "Is that right?"

"It's as close as you can come, I think. But I am also Jessie's servant." Ki smiled a bit sadly. "It is a difficult relationship to explain. I do not question Jessie's orders, or what she does, and she asks nothing about my own personal life. And when the two overlap and mingle, we seem to understand what we do not say."

"It's sort of complicated, all right," Jed agreed. "But I think I follow you."

"Good."

"I still don't understand what this cartel's all about, though," Jed said.

Jessie came into the sitting room. She had changed from her traveling clothes into the skirt and jacket that she wore in town. Hearing Jed's remark about the cartel, she said, "I'll explain as much as I can to you right away, Jed, because you must understand the kind of men we're fighting. But before I get into that, has Ki told you why we came to Virginia City?"

Jed nodded. "We're looking for a fellow named Frank Jeffers. He likes to gamble at the faro tables in the New Ophir Saloon—I guess that'd be one of the fancy ones down by Piper's Opera House, at the other end of C Street. This Jeffers is mixed up in the cartel thing, the way I got it."

"He's probably one of their very important men," Jessie said soberly. "Which makes him very dangerous."

"That doesn't scare me a bit, Jessie," Jed told her. "You don't have to worry about me being afraid to face him down."

"I'm not." Jessie smiled reassuringly, then added, "But don't make the mistake of underestimating the cartel's men, Jed. They're merciless and unscrupulous. If one of them gets you in a corner, kill him before he kills you."

"But the best thing to do is not to let one of them get

151

you cornered," Ki put in. He turned to Jessie and went on, "Should we be getting busy now? The sooner we start—"

"Yes, of course," Jessie replied. "While I was relaxing, I had a few ideas. Let's order lunch sent up, and while we eat, we can talk about them. I'll explain a few things about the cartel to Jed, and then we'll make our plans."

While they ate grilled lake trout taken the afternoon before from the icy depths of nearby Lake Tahoe, Jessie talked about the cartel. Since Jed had been present the night before, when she'd sketched for Governor Kinkead its worldwide organization and sinister motives, she dwelt chiefly on its methods of operation, of which she and Ki had learned the hard way in their earlier encounters.

Without appearing to do so, Jessie covertly studied Jed's handsome bronzed face, freshly shaved after his bath. When she noted how his facial expressions changed in reaction to her explanations, she realized that he was much quicker of mind than she'd thought. With a word added now and then by Ki, she could see when she'd finished that Jed had now begun to comprehend the size and nature of the group behind the South Sierra Railway Company.

"And you think this fellow Jeffers is pretty high up in this cartel outfit?" he asked.

"Very high indeed," Jessie replied. "I'm sure he's Karl Prosser's boss, and that the cartel's put him in full charge of getting the railroad built."

"I'd guess that Jeffers is in charge of a lot more than just the railroad, too," Ki put in. "He's probably the cartel's headman in Nevada Territory, perhaps even more powerful than that."

"You make it sound pretty bad, Ki," Jed frowned. "Isn't the government doing anything? I'd think Congress—"

"Don't depend on Congress," Jessie broke in. "Once a man goes to Congress, he hasn't anything on his mind but getting himself elected again."

"Well, the Secret Service, then," Jed suggested.

"All it can do is try to stop counterfeiters," Jessie told him. "And you've seen right in Hidden Valley how easy it is for the cartel to bribe local sheriffs and judges."

Jed nodded thoughtfully. "I guess that sort of leaves it to people like you and Ki, don't it?"

"We've been fighting them since Father's death, just as he fought them while he was alive," Jessie said.

"Well, you can sure count on me to help you and Ki, Jessie," Jed told her, his voice firm. "That's the kind of outfit that any right-thinking American wants to put out of business!"

"I was sure you'd feel—" Jessie began. She stopped in mid-sentence when raised voices sounded from the hall, followed by the muffled noises of a scuffle.

Ki was at the door before either Jessie or Jed could move. He turned the key quickly and threw the door open. A uniformed bellboy and a man dressed in city-style clothing were grappling with each other. The bellboy was young, and no match for his opponent. As Ki went through the door, the bigger man shoved the bellboy against Ki and started running down the hall.

Ki tried to push the youth out of his way, but the boy was partly stunned, and clung to Ki's arms. The fleeing man reached the end of the corridor and, without breaking stride, dove headfirst through the window that overlooked the back of the hotel building. He disappeared while the tinkling crash of the broken windowpane still hung in the air.

Jed and Jessie reached Ki and pulled the bellboy away from him. Ki ran down the hall at top speed and looked out the broken window. Jed was close behind Ki. Jessie stood in the open door, supporting the dazed bellboy.

One glance out the window told Ki the story. Directly below, the shed roof of the hotel's back entrance stretched only a few feet under the windowsill. The man who'd gone through the window had vanished. Ki and Jed looked down at the hotel's stables, across a narrow courtyard.

"You think he went in there?" Jed asked. "I'm ready to go look and see if we can find him."

Ki shook his head. "He'd be too smart to try and hide. No, Jed. He's gotten away, and he knows exactly where to go, while we're strangers here. Trying to find him would be a waste of time."

They walked back to the open door of the suite. Jessie was talking to the bellboy. She said, "The boy caught whoever it was bending down at the door. He was either trying to pick the lock or listening to us."

Ki nodded, then turned to Jed. "You see that Jessie was not exaggerating when she told you how cunning they are." When Jed started to answer, his question plain in his eyes, Ki shook his head. Indicating the bellboy, he said, "Later, Jed."

Jessie took a double eagle from her pocket and held the gold coin up for the bellboy to see. She said, "This is yours on one condition. You are not to tell anybody about what happened."

"But I've got to report—" the boy began.

"No. You do not have to report. Someone will find the window broken and blame it on a careless guest. But this twenty dollars is yours if you agree to keep absolutely quiet about what happened."

"Well..." The bellboy's eyes were fixed on the gold-piece. He swallowed hard, and nodded. "All right, Miss Johnson. I promise. I swear I won't say a word. Not to the bell captain or the clerk or anybody else."

When the bellboy had left, clutching his double eagle, and the door had been closed and locked again, Jessie said crisply, "They learned we were here sooner than I'd expected, Ki. That means we'll have to work faster than we'd planned. I must send a telegram to the bank in San Francisco right away. While I'm doing that, you and Jed can scout out the New Ophir Saloon."

"But are we—" Jed began.

"We're going through with our plans, Jed," Jessie replied calmly. "We'll just have to be more careful and work faster. Now you and Ki go ahead. I'm going to write my telegram and send it. We don't have any time to waste. With any luck, we'll strike our first blow at the cartel tonight!"

Jessie walked slowly down C Street when she left the hotel. The main thoroughfare was as crowded at ten o'clock at night as it had been in the afternoon when she'd gone to the telegraph office in the Virginia & Truckee Railroad depot, and as it had been in midmorning when she and Ki and Jed had arrived.

Virginia City had two principal industries, silver mining and saloonkeeping, and both operated around the clock. All the retail stores Jessie passed were still open, the saloons that seemed to occupy the ground floor of every second or third building were all busy, and in two or three of the narrow alleys between buildings, where the red lights of the cribs glowed, there were men lined up at some of the doors, waiting for a favorite.

Most of the men on the street seemed to be moving from one saloon to the next, in search of one of the two other recreations the town offered: drinking and gambling. All of them were out looking for a way to forget the past twelve hours or to dull the dread of the next twelve, which they would spend deep in the steam-hot drifts where two or three men were crushed to death each day under collapsing earth. With ten thousand men off-shift and on the streets regardless of the hour, Virginia City quite literally never slept.

When Jessie saw the sign of the New Ophir Saloon just ahead, she began looking for Ki. She was sure he was near, even if he was not visible; Ki was not supposed to be noticed, and she knew there was no one as expert as he in making himself unseen. Just before she reached the busy batwings of the saloon, Jessie opened an unobtrusive door that had

155

a sign in discreetly small letters on its upper panel. The sign did not tell where the door led, but consisted of only two words: LADIES' ENTRANCE.

Ki and Jed had done their work well when they investigated the saloon that afternoon. Jessie knew what lay behind the door. When she entered, she was prepared to walk down the long, carpeted corridor beyond until she reached a second door. This one had no sign. Opening it, Jessie went into the dimly lighted ladies' parlor of the New Ophir.

★

Chapter 15

Jessie had been in ladies' parlors of saloons before, and had found all of them furnished as this one was: there were several small tables, each with a single chair; a large mirror hung on one wall, and the opposite wall had a large plate-glass window opening onto the main barroom; the lighting was dim to the point of obscurity. She was not surprised by the low-turned lamp, and did not turn it higher, as she had learned the reason for the low light.

Saloons of the better class did not admit women, either to drink or to seek a husband who had not come home, so ladies' parlors had two purposes. A woman could sit in the parlor and drink, or, if she stood back from the window opening onto the barroom, the dim light kept her invisible while she looked for an errant husband.

Jessie realized that her arrival must have been signaled by some sort of device that was activated by the parlor door, for she had hardly adjusted the Colt she wore strapped to

157

her hip beneath her green wool suit jacket, shifting it to make her seated position more comfortable, when a silver-haired waiter appeared to take her order.

She asked for a split of champagne, and until the waiter returned with the wine, Jessie was careful to sit with her back to the window that looked into the barroom. After the waiter had opened her champagne and left, she turned to watch the activity in the saloon and at the gaming tables lining its walls.

There were two table layouts on each side, with poker tables between them. Along the wall farthest from Jessie, the games were keno and chuckaluck, and on the near wall, roulette and faro. All of them were busy but not crowded, and Jessie saw Jed at once, standing at the faro table.

Because the New Ophir followed the custom of better-grade saloons and barred from its premises all Indians, Orientals, blacks, and Mexicans, Ki had taken on the job of standing watch outside while Jed looked for Frank Jeffers in the saloon, and Jessie served as his hidden backup. After she'd spotted Jed, Jessie studied the other faro players, but none of them came anywhere close to fitting the somewhat sketchy description of Jeffers that Cheri had given Ki during their pillow talk.

Jessie returned her attention to Jed. He had a small stack of counters in front of him, and she watched him long enough to see that he was betting consistently but conservatively, the way she and Ki had suggested as being the best to avoid attracting attention. Most of Jed's bets were what professional gamblers called "break-eveners," which allowed a player to stretch a small amount of money over a long period of play.

Jessie returned her gaze to Jed now and then while she scanned the crowded barroom, looking for a man who matched the sketchy description that Cheri had given Ki of a tall and distinguished gent with gray hair and mustache, an embroidered vest, a pearl-gray derby, and a diamond stickpin.

Several times as the night wore on, Jessie thought she'd seen Jeffers, but each time the man lacked one or more of the key features for which she was looking. She finished the split of champagne and was considering ordering another when the silver-haired waiter appeared, carrying a tray on which rested a glass of the sparkling wine.

"I didn't order that," Jessie frowned.

"No, ma'am. It's on the house," the waiter said. He smiled conspiratorially as he placed the glass on the table and dropped his voice to a half-whisper. "A customer out in the barroom ordered a fresh bottle, but he was too drunk to finish it. I told the boss there was a lady in here drinking champagne, and he said it'd be all right to bring you this. It'd be a shame just to let it go to waste."

"Of course it would. Thank you," Jessie said.

"When you want to order again, just tap the door. I'll be right close by," the waiter said over his shoulder as he left.

Jessie resumed her watch on the barroom. Jed was still in the same position, and she began studying the faces of the other players. While she watched, Jessie sipped the champagne. It tasted a bit flat, and to finish the wine before it lost its sparkle, she sipped again sooner than she would have done ordinarily, taking a bigger swallow. She replaced the glass on the table and returned her gaze to the window.

There was a constant stream of fresh customers entering and tired or tipsy customers leaving the New Ophir. Though there were many new faces in the barroom, each time Jessie eyed the interior, the men she saw were dressed in everything from shirtsleeves to Prince Albert coats and gates-ajar collars. None of them resembled the description of Frank Jeffers.

Abstractedly, her eyes still fixed on the window, Jessie reached for the glass of champagne. Her arm was slow to respond, and her hand felt cold. Jessie stood up, moving clumsily, her usual quick reflexes sluggish. She realized belatedly that the champagne had been drugged, but while

159

the part of her mind that was still functioning normally told her to get out before it was too late, the part into which the drug had already crept was whispering that it didn't matter much what she did.

Summoning all the inner resources she still controlled, Jessie turned toward the door, supporting herself by leaning on the table. The door opened. The man who stood there wore a gray suit with an embroidered vest, and had a diamond stickpin in his wide cravat and a pearl-gray derby on his head. His chin was cleanshaven, and he had a clipped gray mustache and close-trimmed gray sideburns. He looked at Jessie, who was struggling to maintain her balance, and his cold eyes gleamed like opals reflecting firelight.

At first, Jessie was sure she was suffering from a hallucination. Then the man moved, a quick beckoning gesture to someone behind him. A second man, wide and brawny, came into sight. He held a thick blanket unfolded in his hamlike hands. The two came into the ladies' parlor.

With all the willpower she could muster, Jessie forced her muscles to obey her. She groped for the butt of her Colt with numb and clumsy fingers, but could not push aside the fabric of her coat to get her hand on the weapon. She began to lurch forward, and the hand on which she leaned slid across the table. Her fingers touched something hard and cold.

Jessie was still half-aware of what she was doing. Her hand closed around the empty champagne bottle, and a split second before the two men reached her, she hurled the heavy bottle through the window overlooking the saloon. She heard the crash as the bottle hit the window, and the resonant ringing of the pane shattering. Then the blanket in the hands of the brawny man came down and enveloped her head.

When the champagne bottle crashed through the window, Jed was looking at the faro layout, trying to decide what his next bet should be. The thin ivory counters in his hand clattered to the table as he whirled toward the sound and saw the jagged opening in the window, the bottle in midair, still falling to the floor.

Jed covered the distance to the window in a half-dozen leaping strides, swinging his arms to brush aside the men who were in his path. To get to the window he had to leap to the bar, and as he left his feet, he was drawing his revolver.

Through the jagged triangles of broken glass that still hung in the window frame, he saw the two men in the parlor. One of them was tugging at a blanket that heaved and billowed while he tried to pull it down. The second man stood a short distance from the one with the blanket. He was drawing a snub-nosed, nickel-plated pistol from a shoulder holster.

Jed did not recognize the man in gray as Frank Jeffers. He did not stop to think of each move he was making himself. His instinct took over and he simply acted. Leveling his old-fashioned Cooper Navy revolver, he fired, and while Jeffers's knees began to buckle, Jed put a second bullet into him.

As the cartel boss sprawled limply to the floor, Jed heard the muffled report of another shot and saw the big man holding the blanketed bundle jerk convulsively. Jed fired at the hulking figure. He was dimly aware that the bark of his gun was echoed, but he had no time to think of the echo.

Kicking out the sharp shards of glass that remained in the window frame, Jed jumped into the parlor. Behind him, he was vaguely conscious of the shouts and thudding feet of the men in the saloon, but paid no attention to them.

When Jessie felt the rough fabric of the blanket rasping on her cheeks, she brought around the hand with which she had thrown the bottle and tried to push the blanket away. The man pulling it over her was too strong for her weak, uncoordinated efforts. Jessie was engulfed, her arms pulled down to her sides. She sagged to the floor, and as she felt herself falling, she dropped her hands to break her fall.

161

As she slid through the folds of the blanket, her right hand scraped against the stubby derringer nestled in her boot top. Jessie was clinging desperately to consciousness. She slid the wicked little derringer out, pressed it to the body of the man who was trying to capture her, and pulled the trigger twice. The pressure of her captor's arms relaxed and she fell limply to the floor.

Jed pulled the blanket away and lifted Jessie to her feet. She swayed and leaned against him. Putting an arm around her waist, Jed started helping Jessie to the door. They'd just left the parlor when Ki came running up the corridor. He saw Jed and Jessie, and hurried to help Jed support her. With Jessie sagging between them, they hurried to the street. Behind them, men from the saloon were beginning to trickle into the narrow hall.

In Virginia City, men minded their own business, especially after midnight. No one turned to look at Ki and Jed while they walked to the International Hotel, supporting Jessie's sagging form between them. The desk clerk did not change expression when the trio passed through the lobby and entered the elevator. The hall was deserted. Jed supported Jessie while Ki unlocked the door. They carried her inside and lowered her to the sofa.

Her brief trip in the brisk night had partially revived her. Jessie opened her eyes and saw Ki. In a thick, slow voice, she said, "Oh—Ki—That was Frank Jeffers who—"

"Yes, I know," Ki replied. "He's dead, Jessie."

"Did I shoot him, Ki? I think I fired the derringer."

Jed said, "I shot him, Jessie."

"Oh. Thank you, Jed..." she mumbled.

"He was about to shoot me," Jed said. "But I shot first."

Jed's forehead crinkled into a frown, as though saying the words had only now brought home to him what he'd done. He stood for a moment, staring into space. Then he went to one of the armchairs and sat down, his eyes fixed on the wall.

Ki understood Jed's emotions, and knew that the young man needed action to get his mind off himself. He said briskly, "We must help Jessie get rid of the drugs they've given her, Jed. Go in her bathroom and fill the tub with cold water. I'm going down to the desk and get some ice and coffee."

At the desk, waiting for the ice and coffee he'd ordered, Ki had a sudden thought. When the bellboy brought his order, Ki said to the clerk, "I want to rent the room across the hall from Miss Johnson's suite for tonight."

His face expressionless, the clerk nodded, turned to the pigeonholes behind the desk, and handed over the key. Ki carried the ice and coffee upstairs. Jed had filled the bathtub and now stood by the divan, looking at Jessie. Her eyes were closed and she was breathing deeply.

"Rub her face with some ice while I get her boots off," Ki told Jed. "As soon as she's able to move, she can get into the tub. I don't know what kind of drug she's been given, but she's not really knocked out, just groggy."

A few minutes after Ki and Jed began their ministrations, Jessie opened her eyes and looked at them. "I—I think I'm all right now," she said. "Thank you both for taking care of me."

"There's a tub of cold water waiting for you," Ki told her. "And I don't think we'll need to worry about the cartel trying to get to us tonight, here in the hotel."

Jessie was sitting up now. She nodded her agreement and said, "They'll be too disorganized after Jeffers's death."

"Just in case they should try something," Ki went on, "I'll be in the room across the hall, with the door opened a crack. Jed will stay here in the sitting room."

Stretched out in the bathtub, Jessie soaked in the cold water until her head cleared and her muscles regained their tone. After draining the tub, she refilled it with warm water and soaped her body, then rinsed away the soap, rubbing herself with the washrag until her skin tingled. Once more herself, feeling the familiar surge of vitality that always

163

followed a safe escape from danger, she stopped in the bedroom long enough to slip on a silk dressing gown and brush her mane of tawny gold hair until it glowed, then she went into the sitting room.

Jed sat on the divan, his Cooper Navy revolver beside him. He looked up and saw Jessie, the thin silk robe emphasizing rather than hiding the lush contours of her body. He stared at Jessie until he saw the beginning of a smile twitch her lips. In sudden embarrassment, he looked away and asked quickly, "How do you feel now, Jessie?"

"Wonderful, Jed!" she smiled. "With Frank Jeffers dead, we can all breathe a lot easier."

"I wish I felt good about it," Jed said. "I never killed a man before, Jessie. I've got a funny, sad kind of feeling."

"Don't think about it, then," she said. She indicated the pistol on the sofa. "You can put that away, Jed. Ki was right, we won't have any more trouble tonight."

Jed started to holster the gun, then realized he'd taken off his gunbelt, and laid the pistol on the floor. Jessie sat down beside him.

"Jeffers was an important link in the cartel," she said. "We broke it when you shot him. He can't be replaced soon."

"You sound like you're glad I had to shoot him!"

"No, not glad. But not sorry, either. With Jeffers dead, we can straighten things out faster in Hidden Valley."

"Are we going back there right away?"

Jessie shook her head. "Not today, perhaps not tomorrow. I wired my bank in San Francisco for information about Oscar Breyer and the Hidden Valley bank, and told them to send a man here with it. He ought to be here today, though."

His voice both thoughtful and puzzled, Jed said, "You know, I want to go back to the valley, but I don't want to. It's been real exciting being with you and Ki, tonight especially."

"I'm still tense and a little shaky, though." Jessie put her

164

hand on Jed's. "You can feel my hands tremble now and then."

"They don't feel shaky to me," Jed told her. He took both her hands in his. "I like the way they feel, Jessie."

"I feel better with you holding them," Jessie said.

She let her arms sag slowly, pulling her clasped hands down to rest on her thigh. Jed looked at her, his face puzzled, but with the hint of a question in his eyes.

Jessie leaned back, resting her head on the divan, and turned her face to him. Jed hesitated for only a moment, then he bent to kiss her. She parted her lips and caressed his closed lips with the tip of her tongue, and his tongue slid out to meet hers.

For a moment they stayed motionless. Jessie was the first to move. She slipped one of her hands free and brushed her palm along Jed's thigh until she found the firm bulge that was beginning to stretch the cloth of his trousers. With her other hand she guided Jed's hands to her breasts. He hesitated briefly, then closed them over the warm, inviting globes.

Jessie kept passing her hand back and forth along Jed's erection, feeling him grow yet firmer under her caress. Jed's callused fingers closed on her breasts with a firmness that was almost painful, yet set her whole body to tingling as though tiny, invisible sparks were bursting inside her. She broke their prolonged kiss and looked up into Jed's startled face.

"Ki won't disturb us for a long time," she said softly. "And we'll be more comfortable in the bedroom."

Jed needed no further encouragement. He picked Jessie up and carried her through the open bedroom door.

He started for the bed, but Jessie shook her head. Jed relaxed his arms and let her feet swing to the floor. Jessie pulled the knotted cord that belted her robe, and shrugged it off. Jed stared at her for a moment, her body glowing in the soft light that spilled in through the door from the sitting room.

She began unbuckling his belt, fumbling in the dimness, and Jed moved to help her. He levered off his boots and kicked them aside, then his hands tangled with Jessie's as he tried to get out of his trousers, shirt, and balbriggans all at the same time. Jessie's hands brushed Jed's as together they pulled the layers of clothing down over his hips.

Their eager fumbling ended quickly. When the encumbering balbriggans slid down Jed's thighs and Jessie saw his rigid shaft spring up invitingly, she let him kick his legs free, and with both hands she encircled the sturdy cylinder of pulsing flesh.

Jed gasped when he felt her warm hands grasping him. Too impatient now to wait, he lifted Jessie by the waist and, with one long stride, carried her to the bed. She sank back and parted her thighs, and when Jed bent over her, Jessie grasped his shaft again and guided him to the moist warmth that was awaiting him.

Now it was Jessie who gasped with a throaty whimper of joy when she felt Jed sliding in to fill her. She did not try to control herself.

Locking her feet behind Jed's hips, she pulled him deeper. Her hips rolled and her body writhed in quickly mounting ecstasy, and she let herself go almost as soon as he began thrusting into her with firm, hard strokes.

"Oh, wonderful, Jed!" Jessie gasped, her words blurred softly between the soft cries that bubbled from her throat as she rocked beneath him. "Go slower now. I want you in me for a long, long time!"

Jed did not answer, nor did he stop when the soft cries of joy poured from her throat, but he slowed his stroking to a more leisurely tempo. Looking up at his bronzed young face, Jessie saw that his eyes were closed, his lips parted in a smile. Jessie closed her own eyes and abandoned herself to enjoyment.

Far sooner than she'd expected, her sensations began to build again. Jed was panting now, thrusting faster, his arms beginning to tremble. Jessie raised her hips higher and bent

166

her knees, spread her thighs even wider, opening herself to accept Jed's lunges.

"Faster, Jed!" she urged. "I want to go with you!"

"Yes. But I'm almost there, Jessie," he panted.

Jessie still needed more time. Arching her back, she raised her hips to increase the friction of Jed's driving shaft against her swollen bud. Above her, Jed was gasping each time he plunged into her, and Jessie felt his hips beginning to tremble. She sprawled her thighs wide to let him go deeper, and felt her own urge mounting.

Jed was very close now, and Jessie let herself ride with him to the final shuddering moments when neither could endure the joyous pain of self-control for another instant. They flowed together and lay with slack muscles shaken by their spasmodic shuddering, which diminished bit by bit and finally ended.

Jed moved as though to leave her, but Jessie stopped him.

"No," she said. "Not yet."

"But I'm too heavy to lay here on you," Jed protested.

"Then we'll roll over, and I'll lie on you."

In their new position, still connected by their bond of flesh, Jessie soon began caressing Jed by first firming and then relaxing her inner muscles. This was but one of many things she'd been taught by the wise old geisha, Myobu, in whose charge her father had placed Jessie after her mother's death.

Jed's young virility led him to respond quickly. Jessie rose to her knees, straddled him, and continued the soft caresses until Jed was fully erect. Then she began rocking back and forth in a steady, insinuating rhythm, keeping herself taut, her muscles grasping and releasing, until Jed's eyes squeezed shut and his hips heaved up as he tried to thrust deeper into her. Jessie moved faster and faster and increased the soft friction of her caresses until they joined again in frantic spasms that left them even more satisfied than they had been before.

When strength flowed back to them, Jed said, "There's not a thing I'd like more than to stay just like we are, Jessie. But it's getting light outside and Ki's going to be coming back."

"I don't want to move, either," Jessie whispered. "But I know we've got to." They rolled apart reluctantly. Jessie went on, "This isn't the last time we'll find to be together, Jed. Getting things straightened up in Hidden Valley will take time, and I'm not in a hurry now. We'll be together again soon, I promise you."

"It can't be too soon," he replied. "I don't think I'd ever get enough of you, Jessie, but I do know one thing. I'd sure like to try."

★
Chapter 16

Jessie, Ki, and Jed sat pleasantly relaxed at the table in the suite's sitting room, following a late breakfast. Jessie was holding the sheaf of papers that had arrived from Carson City by the morning mail.

"Governor Kinkead gave us a bit more than we asked for, Ki," she said as she refolded the papers and laid them down. "He's commissoned Captain Bob a colonel in the territorial militia, and in his letter he says the Captain can raise a volunteer force any time an emergency threatens the peace in Hidden Valley."

"We're going to be legal for a change, then." Ki smiled. "It's good to have someone else on our side, isn't it?"

"If I know the Captain, he'd have done that without waiting for the governor to tell him he could," Jed commented. "And I'd be the first one to—" He stopped short as a knock on the door brought them all to their feet in nervous reaction from the events of the night just ended.

There was a second knock, more prolonged than the first.

Jessie said, "I don't think we need to worry, but—"

She went into the bedroom and came back carrying her Colt. Holding the pistol by her side, she stood against the wall beside the door and nodded to Ki. He opened the door. The man who stood waiting was young and clean-shaven. The tailoring of his suit, a strangely harmonious blend of French and British styles, was unique to San Francisco. He carried a leather briefcase.

"Is this Miss Jessica Starbuck's suite?" he asked. When Ki nodded, he handed over the card he held ready in his hand and asked, "Will you please announce me, then?"

Ki glanced at the card, which read *Arthur V. Barston III, Vice-president, First California Bank*. Ki handed the card to Jessie, and after glancing at it, she dropped the Colt on the chair by the door and stepped around to greet the somewhat bewildered visitor.

"Come in, Mr. Barston," Jessie said, extending her hand. "We're just having after-breakfast coffee. Won't you join us?"

Barston came in. Making only a token effort to conceal his curiosity, he looked at Ki again, then at Jed, and finally turned back to Jessie.

"I would like coffee very much, Miss Starbuck," he said. "I've just made my first trip on the Virginia & Truckee railroad, and it's not an experience for which I was prepared."

"I've heard there are a few curves in the tracks," Jessie commented with a smile. She indicated a chair, and Barston sat down. He held his briefcase on his lap, and put his hat on the floor beside him. Ki handed him a cup of coffee. Jessie went on, "It's kind of you to make such a long trip, Mr. Barston. It was the only way I could be sure that the information you brought would be kept confidential and delivered promptly."

"Oh, of course, Miss Starbuck. And even if you weren't a very substantial stockholder in the First California, we

170

would have been glad to comply with any reasonable request." Barston opened his briefcase and took out a sheaf of papers. He went on, "In your situation, though, it seems a bit strange that you should ask for information of this kind."

Jessie frowned. "I'm afraid I don't follow you."

"You inquired as to the ownership of the stock in the bank in Hidden Valley, here in Nevada Territory, did you not?"

"Yes. Why is that strange? I wanted the information and asked for it. Who does own the bank, Mr. Barston?"

"You do, Miss Starbuck," Barston replied.

Jessie opened her mouth to say something, but thought better of it, closed her mouth, and swallowed hard. She recovered from the shock quickly and asked, "How could I own it and know nothing about it?"

"That is understandable," Barston said pontifically. "Our bank has been acting as your agent and trustee in managing the Hidden Valley bank's affairs. In going through the old records, I learned that the arrangement was made by your father. During his lifetime, he found no reason to give us specific instructions, so all the documents and records have been accumulating in our files as he wished. Yes, I can see why you'd have no knowledge of it."

"But if I give you instructions now—" Jessie began.

"They will most certainly be followed, Miss Starbuck."

"Without having to change my father's arrangement?"

"There's no reason to disturb it that I can see."

"Very well," Jessie said. "I have only one instruction. I want you to fire Oscar Breyer today and hire a new manager."

Barston made no comment, but looked expectantly at Jessie. When she gave no indication of continuing, he asked, "What reason am I to give Mr. Breyer for discharging him, Miss Starbuck?"

"You don't—" Jessie began, then a flicker of a smile stole over her face. "Don't give him a reason, Mr. Barston.

171

But some time after he's been fired, let him find out I own the bank."

"If those are your instructions, we will follow them, Miss Starbuck. And the new manager?"

"Your people can select him," Jessie shrugged. "But, Mr. Barston, do put a man in charge who's honest, and who understands that small farmers and ranchers have special problems. If you do that, I won't trouble you with any more odd requests."

His voice puzzled, Barston asked, "You don't want to see the bank's financial statement? Its earning records? Its—"

"I'll leave those things to you, Mr. Barston." Jessie stood up. "Thank you very much for the special service."

Before the bewildered banker quite understood what was happening, Ki had ushered him out of the suite and closed the door. Jessie, Ki, and Jed exchanged wide smiles.

Jed said, "You know, Jessie, you've got a way of cutting right down to the bone when you set out to do something. I never saw anybody get a job finished so quick."

"That's a nice thing to say, Jed, but our job's not finished yet," Jessie reminded him. "Frank Jeffers must have given Prosser orders, and a very free hand in carrying them out."

"But Jeffers is dead!" Jed exclaimed.

"Yes," Ki replied. "But Prosser doesn't know that."

Jessie said, "The cartel's like a snake, Jed. It lives a long time, even after its head's been cut off. We've got to get back to Hidden Valley as fast as we can, and stop Karl Prosser from carrying out Jeffers's orders."

"Well, I got to admit the last part of that ride was real fine, but I sure wouldn't want to take the first part again soon," Jed said.

He and Jessie and Ki stood by the railroad siding in the bright afternoon sun, watching the caboose of the Central Pacific freight train diminishing in the distance.

Because there'd been no need to return by way of Carson

172

City, they'd saved a day in the saddle by taking the swaying, curve-beset Virginia & Truckee train from Virginia City, their horses riding in a stock car. At the junction east of Truckee, they'd switched to the CP, which had dropped them at the spur built by the South Sierra Railway Company to handle its shipments of material. A long ride still lay ahead of them, but traveling by train had cut in half the time required for their return trip.

"If we're going to get to Hidden Valley by midnight, we'd better start riding," Jessie told her companions. Setting an example, she swung nimbly into the saddle and the trio started the last leg of their return trip.

Although they'd saved time on the train, the trip from the siding to the valley was a long one. They stopped only when it was necessary to rest the horses, and wasted no time cooking, but made a supper from crusty Basque bread and piquant sausage that they ate in the saddle. The ride would have been much longer had they not been able to keep the horses on the strip of level ground beside the railroad spur. Even so, they'd been riding in darkness for what seemed an interminable time before they reached the end of the tracks laid for the cartel's railroad.

"It's downhill all the rest of the way now," Jed said encouragingly. "And we'll make good time, because I know every inch of the trail we'll be traveling over."

A sliver of moon had shown up shortly before they passed the track end, and its faint rays provided enough light for Jed to keep on the trail. They reached the north pass, and though none of them sighed audibly, they felt a surge of relief when they saw the widely separated glowing pinpoints in the night that marked farm houses, and the miniature galaxy of brighter dots that twinkled from the town.

They'd ridden only a short distance toward the clustered lights when Jessie spoke. "Ki, Jed, it's just occurred to me. Doesn't it seem odd that so many people are up as late as this, in a farming town like Hidden Valley?"

Jed spoke quickly. "I haven't thought about it, Jessie,

173

but it's sure not usual. My folks go to bed before nine, every night except church meeting nights."

"Something has happened," Ki said. "Perhaps we have gotten back just in time."

There was no way to get more speed from the weary horses. They let the animals set the pace, and held back their impatience until they reached the town. Without discussion, they turned into the street leading to Captain Tinker's house. Even before they reached the house, they could see that it was ablaze with light. A buggy, a wagon, and several horses in front of the house kept them from riding to the door. They pulled up, dropped the reins over their horses' heads, and hurried inside.

Captain Tinker sat in the dining room behind a table covered with papers. Several men sat around the big table; Jessie recognized the faces of two of them, but could not remember their names. The Captain looked up when she and Ki and Jed stopped in the doorway, and slapped his hand on table.

"Jessie!" he exclaimed. "I'm real glad to see you, and maybe a mite gladder to see Ki and Jed! Not that you aren't welcome back, Jessie, but we need men, every one we can muster up!"

"When you say 'muster,' Captain, you give me the idea you're getting ready to fight a war," Jessie said, holding her curiosity in check and keeping her voice calm.

"You might say we are," the Captain replied. "Prosser's come out in the open now, and there's hell to pay, Jessie. I know you're all tired, riding in from Carson City, but pull up a chair and I'll tell you what we're up against."

"Let me tell you the good news first," Jessie suggested. "The man who was the real boss of this railroad is dead. There won't be a South Sierra Railway Company within a few weeks. The governor is putting through a bill for a special election, so you'll be rid of your crooked county officials too."

"That's the best thing I've heard since this mess started,"

the Captain said. "But I don't see that it's going to help us much right now. Go on and sit down, because we're going to have to do some talking, Jessie, as well as some tall figuring, if we expect to stop this war the railroad's started."

While they were getting settled, Jed asked anxiously, "You mean there's been open fighting, Captain?"

"Some. But there's certain to be more."

"I hope nobody's been hurt," Jed frowned. "Daddy's all right, isn't he? And Blaine, how about him?"

"Your folks are all right, Jed," the Captain replied. "And Blaine's out keeping an eye on things right now. But Jethro Garvey's been killed, and I imagine we haven't seen the worst of it yet."

"Suppose you explain what's happened, Captain," Ki suggested. "We're all very curious."

"It started the day after you left here," the Captain said. "About sunset, men started drifting into town. Riders. All of them rough lookers, all of them wearing pistol belts and carrying rifles. We didn't pay much attention at first, but pretty soon somebody remarked that they all went to that rooming house next to the saloon, and it looked like they were settling in to stay."

"How many?" Jessie asked tersely.

"We don't know for sure, Jessie. Thirty, maybe more."

Jessie nodded, and Captain Tinker went on with his story. "We didn't think much of it, even then, until Karl Prosser rode out with five of the scoundrels to the Garvey place. There were a bunch of men from town there, a half-dozen or so, trying to get started building a new house for Jethro and Rose. Prosser made them another bid to buy, and Jethro kept saying no. Then Prosser told the rascals with him to get busy, and they held the Garveys and others at gunpoint and burned all the lumber that Jethro'd gotten together for his new house."

"It wasn't such a much of lumber," one of the men at the table put in when Tinker paused. "All that most of us could give them was what we had left around our own places, odds and ends of stuff. But it was all Jethro had to start building with."

"Well," the Captain resumed, "Jethro got mad and rushed the gang, and one of them shot him. Then they set fire to the lumber and rode off. And that was when we got our dander up." He turned from Jessie to the man across the table from him. "You were with Blaine at the saloon, Stewart. Tell Jessie about it."

"There's not a lot to tell," Stewart said. "Blaine rounded up five of us and we went to the saloon. Only we didn't come close to getting there. That bunch has turned the saloon and the rooming house into a fort, Miss Jessie. They started shooting as soon as we got in rifle range. We didn't press our luck, so nobody got hurt. We didn't even fire a shot, because they were shooting from inside and we couldn't see anybody to shoot at."

"It'll take an army to get them out of there, Jessie," the Captain said. "The saloon's got its own well, and I'd bet a plug of tobacco to a double eagle they've got all the food they need."

"You've got the authority to raise an army if you want to, Captain," Jessie said. "Governor Kinkead's made you a colonel in the territorial militia."

"That was a nice thing for John to do," Tinker said. "But I don't see that it's going to help us much, except to make us legal."

While they'd talked, the room had gradually grown brighter. The lamplight was paling as gray dawn light crept through the windows, heralding the sunrise.

Ki said, "Those buildings must have a vulnerable spot somewhere, Jessie. I've only seen them from inside, but I'd like to go scout around down there before the light gets better."

"I don't know that it'll do any good," the Captain said. "I guess if you're going, I'll go along. I'd like to talk to Blaine and see if anything's happened during the night."

176

● ● ●

They saw Blaine Abel standing in front of the courthouse, and Captain Tinker pulled up the wagon. Abel came over to them, and Ki and Jed dismounted to join him at the buggy.

"It's been quiet," Abel said, anticipating their questions. "A couple of the boys and I scouted up close to the buildings last night, but we didn't find out much. We saw gun muzzles poking out the windows all around the rooming house, and they've cut rifle ports in the fences between it and the saloon. There were so many men around the saloon, we couldn't get very close to it, but from the looks of things, they mean business."

"There was never any doubt of that," Jessie said. "Even if we told them that the man who's the real boss of this railroad scheme is dead now, and the railroad is too, they'd think we were just trying to trick them, and wouldn't believe us."

"Is that right, Captain?" Abel asked.

"If Jessie says it is, you can take it for gospel, Blaine," Tinker replied. "And I'll put in with what she just got through saying, too. Prosser doesn't know yet what's happened, and he won't believe anything we try to tell him. He'll think we're just spinning a tall yarn, trying to talk him into giving up."

"I don't see how we can get him and that bunch of toughs out of that place without a lot of men getting hurt, then," Abel said. "It would take a cannon to roust them out."

Discouragement in his voice, the Captain said, "The only way we could get a cannon is to call in the army, and that'd take a month. There's not a fort left in the territory now."

Jessie had been listening, her keen mind weighing possibilities, and discarding each one as it occurred to her. She shifted her position on the hard seat of the buggy and stretched, throwing back her head to ease the muscles that were aching after her long night in the saddle. The sun was rising now, its low golden rays bathing the courthouse square. She blinked, and turned to the two discouraged men.

"We don't have to ask the army for a cannon," she told them quietly. "We've got one right here. All we have to do is figure out how to use it."

All of them turned to follow Jessie's pointing finger. They saw the small brass Fremont cannon standing on it low pedestal in front of the courthouse, a pyramid of cannonballs embedded in mortar beside it. In the morning sun, the cannon's brass barrel showed a dark brown from lack of polishing.

"You mean that little thing?" Captain Tinker snorted. "It hasn't been fired since we quit having Fourth of July blowouts when the War started, and all we shot in it then was wadding."

"It would still shoot, wouldn't it?" Jessie asked. "Those cannonballs fit it, don't they? And there should be plenty of gunpowder at the stores."

"Oh, it'll fire," the Captain said. "There's nothing about that kind of cannon to go wrong. Ream out the touchhole and put in the powder and ball, and it'll shoot, all right."

"Then what are we waiting for?" she asked.

Getting the cannon ready took most of the morning. There were a lot of small jobs to be done: cleaning the bore, reaming the touchhole, making a ramrod, putting powder in bags, tearing up old rags for wadding, scraping the cannonballs clean of the mortar in which they'd been embedded, improvising a carriage from scraps of timber. The individual jobs were small, though, and there was no lack of volunteers. News of Jethro Garvey's murder had spread, and the Hidden Valley men were boiling with anger.

Blaine Abel posted guards out of rifle range around the saloon and the rooming house, to keep the hired guns confined to the buildings. The gunmen fired a warning shot or two at the sentries, but made no real effort to break out.

"They're waiting for dark," Captain Tinker said during

178

one of the pauses during the job of putting the cannon in shape. "They might be able to break out, too, if we don't stop them first."

"We'll be ready in another two hours, Captain," Ki said. "But ever since Jessie got this idea, I've been wondering where we're going to find a cannoneer."

"You're looking at him, Ki," Tinker replied. "I was a right fair ship's gunner's mate before I got my master mariner's certificate. It's been many a year, but I don't think I've forgotten anything."

News of what was happening had spread quickly through the valley, and the square was crowded when the willing volunteers rolled the little brass cannon into the position the Captain had chosen. The sun was noontime high. The polished barrel of the cannon tossed back its rays as Captain Tinker propped himself up on his cane and leaned over to sight the target.

If the cartel's hired gunmen had noticed the activity in the street beyond the saloon, they had not tried to interfere. When he was sure that his elevation was correct, the captain pushed himself erect and nodded to Blaine Abel.

"We'll give them one chance to throw out their guns and come out and surrender," he told Abel. "If they don't, you scoot back out of range, and I'll touch her off."

"Be sure to tell Prosser that his boss is dead," Jessie reminded Abel. "He won't believe you, but tell him anyhow."

Abel nodded. He took a fresh white handkerchief from his pocket and began waving it as he walked toward the saloon. Karl Prosser came out on the veranda, followed by a half-dozen of the gunmen. They carried rifles, and held them ready as they bunched up behind him.

Abel stopped and called out, "Prosser, we're giving you and your men one chance to surrender. Your boss in Virginia City is dead. The railroad's dead too. Cut your losses and give up!"

"Talk's cheap, Abel!" Prosser replied. "You think I'm

179

fool enough to swallow your lying bullshit, but you're wrong! If you want us out, come and get us!"

"One chance is all you get, Prosser!" Abel warned.

"I'll tell you again," Prosser retorted. "Come in and get us, if you've got the guts!"

For a full minute, a minute that seemed an hour, the two stared at one another. Jessie and Ki, standing beside Captain Tinker at the cannon, exchanged looks as Abel finally turned away and began walking back down the sunbathed street.

Jessie said, "That's about what we expected, Captain. We gave them their chance. It's up to you and the cannon, now."

The Captain nodded. "I'm ready, Jessie. Soon as Blaine's out of rifle range, I'll touch it off."

When the cannon was finally fired, its report was disappointingly flat. It sounded like a big firecracker, but the ball it lofted to the gunmen's refuge landed true. It crashed into the front of the saloon just above the awning, and even in the square, the noise of wood cracking and splintering was impressive.

A ragged volley of rifle shots from the rooming house rang out from the men holed up there, but the cannon was well beyond rifle range. The rifle slugs raised dust from the street, but had no other effect.

"You're aiming for the rooming house now?" Jessie asked as Ki and Jed rushed up to shift the cannon in line with Captain Tinker's leveled cane.

"I'll put a ball into it dead amidships," the old man answered, bending to adjust the gun's leveling screw.

If the effects of the first cannonball had been impressive, those of the second were even more so. The shot tore into the center of the tall building, and almost at once the roof began to sag. Another ball into the saloon brought the gunmen pouring out like ants, their hands raised. Blaine Abel and his deputies, their rifles leveled, went to meet them.

"I don't think you'll need to fire again, Captain," Jessie

180

said as they watched the Hidden Valley men disarming the cartel thugs and binding their wrists.

"I guess it's just as well, Jessie," the Captain replied. "Look here." He pointed to the cannon's breech. A wide crack ran along the top of the barrel from the touchhole almost to the muzzle. "Looks like Fremont's cannon's let off its last ball."

"It won the railroad war for us, though," Jessie said. She smiled as she turned to Ki. "And we can depend on the Captain to do whatever else is needed. Ki, as long as we're so close to the stagecoach station, why don't we walk down there and find out when we can take the next stage that will get us started back to the Circle Star?"

The hottest trio in Western history is riding your way in these giant LONGARM adventures!

The matchless lawman LONGARM teams up with the fabulous duo Jessie and Ki of LONE STAR fame for exciting Western tales that are not to be missed!

____ 07386-5   LONGARM AND THE LONE STAR LEGEND $2.95

____ 07085-8   LONGARM AND THE LONE STAR VENGEANCE $2.95